DANNY ORLIS
AND THE MYSTERY AT SMUGGLER'S POINT

DANNY ORLIS AND THE MYSTERY AT SMUGGLER'S POINT

BERNARD PALMER

Danny Orlis and the Mystery at Smuggler's Point
© 2023 by Bernard Palmer
All rights reserved. First edition 1956.
Second edition 2023.

Cover image: Adobe Firefly
Character illustrations: John Ball
Editors: Jon D. Fogdall and Ruth Clark

Aneko Press Youth
www.anekopress.com
Aneko Press, Life Sentence Publishing, and our logos are trademarks of Life Sentence Publishing, Inc.
203 E. Birch Street
P.O. Box 652
Abbotsford, WI 54405
JUVENILE FICTION / Religious / Christian / Action & Adventure
Paperback ISBN: 978-1-62245-954-4
eBook ISBN: 978-1-62245-955-1
10 9 8 7 6 5 4 3 2
Available where books are sold

CONTENTS

Ch. 1: The Stranger 1

Ch. 2: The Ill-Tempered Tom LeFevre 13

Ch. 3: The Man in the Bush 23

Ch. 4: Danny to the Rescue....................................33

Ch. 5: Has Somebody Got It in for You? 43

Ch. 6: Peter's New Boat...53

Ch. 7: The Lonely Boy 63

Ch. 8: The Old Ways 75

Ch. 9: Stay Away from Orlis 87

Ch. 10: Somebody's Out There................................97

Ch. 11: Accused..107

Ch. 12: "It Couldn't Have Been Danny"..................117

Ch. 13: Exposed..129

CHAPTER 1

THE STRANGER

The *Island Queen* slowed at the mouth of Pine Creek, her bow settling into the choppy water. As she turned toward the Orlis dock, the horn sounded. Danny Orlis got to his feet and peered through the curtains at the sleek little boat that was nosing toward the dock after making its way across the Big Traverse from Warroad.

"They're here, Dad!" he called out.

Carl Orlis, who had been working on his books, joined his son, and they went out the door and down to the dock together. It had been only a week since Danny and Jim had returned from Mexico. Both boys had been very busy. Danny was helping his dad at their little fishing camp at Angle Inlet. He had mowed the lawn, put a new roof on one of the tourist cabins, and helped his dad repair the dock, while Jim had returned to his job as helper on the *Island Queen*.

Now, however, Danny was going to get another break. His cousin, Grant Hood, from Colorado, was coming out to spend three or four weeks before school started. Danny was elected to show him around and see that he had a good time. Danny had visited his cousin once several years before, but this would be Grant's first trip to the Northwest Angle.

"What if he doesn't like it here, Dad?" Danny asked only that morning.

"He'll like it, all right."

"Some guys don't."

Carl Orlis nodded. "We'll cross that bridge when we come to it."

Several paces from the water's edge, Danny stopped and watched as Jim leaped nimbly to the pier and secured the line around a cleat. A stocky, broad-shouldered boy about Danny's own age was standing in the fantail, poised as though he, too, was about to jump to the dock. He caught sight of Danny and waved. Danny waved in reply and burst onto the dock—almost colliding with Jim, who by that time was securing the stern line.

"Hey, Man! Watch it!"

"Sorry, dude." Danny put up his hands quickly, as though to catch Jim if he knocked him off balance. After a moment he turned to his cousin.

"Hi," he said self-consciously. "How're you doin'?"

"We've been doing great!" Jim broke in. "Grant's

a cool guy! Wish I could stay up here with you. We'd have a blast."

"No way," his grandfather broke in. "You've done enough gallivanting this summer. You're going to work with me on the *Queen*."

"I know, I know," Jim repeated quickly. "That was our deal when you let me off to go to Mexico."

Danny helped Grant carry his gear to the little tourist cabin where the two of them would be staying. "You can get your stuff unpacked, Grant," he said. "I'll be back in a little while."

His cousin frowned. "What're you going to do?"

"Cap and Jim have a lot of freight this afternoon," Danny explained. "I thought I'd go and help them unload."

"Is there any reason why I can't go, too?" Grant wanted to know. "They might need an extra pair of hands."

"You can come if you want to."

"Sounds good," his cousin said. "We'll get the work done. Then we can *all* take it easy."

Danny Orlis nodded, approval gleaming in his bronzed features. He liked his cousin more now than he had the last time they were together. He acted as though he wasn't afraid to do his part, even when it came to work. If that kept up, Danny knew that he and Grant would get along fine—and it did. As soon as the *Island Queen* stopped at one of the places along the lake where Cap had freight to leave, Grant was there—helping in every way he could.

When they got back from delivering the lumber and supplies to some of the other residents of the Angle, Danny was more excited about his cousin than ever. Grant not only pitched in and worked—he was also well-liked by the men and boys where they stopped. It looked as though it was going to be a great three weeks.

They got the freight delivered in record time and were on their way back to the Orlis home. "I ought to have all three of you working for me," Cap said as they approached the dock. "I wouldn't have to do anything except take in the money."

"That would suit me," Jim said.

Grant turned to Danny. "Is that as much fun as fishing?" he asked, trying to sound as though he thought Cap was serious.

"Not quite."

"Then I think maybe I'd rather fish. Ever since you and your parents visited us, I've been dreaming about getting up here so I could catch some of those big northerns and walleyes that are supposed to be here."

"They're here, all right," Cap told him. "And you couldn't have a better guide than Danny."

Carl Orlis was on shore when the boys and Jim's grandfather got off the boat. Usually he was smiling, but that afternoon a scowl darkened his mild features.

"Danny," he said seriously, "after supper I'd like to have you and Grant take the motors off the boats and put them in the shed so they can be locked up."

Questions narrowed Danny's eyes, but he did not voice them right then. He figured if his dad wanted to explain, he would do so without prodding.

"Sounds like you've been talkin' to Ivar Sherwood," Cap said.

Mr. Orlis nodded. "He stopped by while you were gone. Wanted to know if we'd missed anything the last few nights."

"I know. I talked to him at American Point earlier today. Said he had a net and half a dozen traps stolen."

"It's *got* to be somebody from the outside," Mr. Orlis continued. "We don't have trouble like that unless someone who comes in does it. We've *never* had to lock things more than a few nights in all the years I've been here."

When Danny learned that his mom didn't have supper ready, he found his dad and asked if they should start taking the motors to the shed immediately.

"It doesn't make any difference to me," Carl told him, "but you ought to talk to Keeler and his party before you remove the motor from the boat he's been using. They might want to go out on the lake again this evening."

"I'll check," Danny said, "but I don't think they are. They just got in a little while ago and are in the filleting shed cleaning fish. It looks as though they'll be there for a while."

The fishermen didn't plan on going out again that night, so, with Jim's help, Danny and Grant removed their motor first. They balanced it in the wheelbarrow and took it to the shed behind the house.

"Back home," Grant said as they put the last outboard into the shed and closed the heavy padlock in the hasp, "we wouldn't be able to leave *anything* out—even for a few hours. Someone would be sure to walk away with it."

"People aren't like that up here," Jim replied. "Mostly, they're honest and wouldn't take anything that didn't belong to them."

Mary Orlis called them to supper just then, and the boys went into the kitchen to wash up. By the time they went into the dining room, everyone else was at the table. Keeler and his fishing buddies were sitting along one side and an end next to Cap and Jim. Mr. and Mrs. Orlis, Danny, and his cousin filled the rest of the chairs.

"What's going on around here today?" Keeler asked curiously. "You've never locked anything before."

"We haven't had to," Carl told him. "But there must be a thief around now. One of the fishermen on the Canadian side was over a little while ago. A thief broke into his storage shed last night and stole one of his nets and some traps. He came over to warn us so we could lock things up for a time—until the guy is caught. I think you'd better lock your cabin, too."

"Even when we come up here for meals?"

He nodded. "It would be easy for someone to come up the creek by boat, approaching the cabins from that side. He could ransack the place, and we'd never know it."

By this time, all other conversation at the table had stopped. "Think he'll head this way?" Keeler persisted.

Danny's dad shrugged. "I don't have a clue. Ivar Sherwood does live quite a distance from here, but anybody with a fast engine could make it in a little while." He paused briefly. "We'd better be careful until we know for sure that the guy's been caught or has left the country."

After Carl had Jim ask the blessing and the food was served, the group at the table began to talk about the prospects for good hunting in the fall. Inevitably the conversation drifted to the fishing Keeler and his friends had been doing. It had always been good at Angle Inlet every time they had been there, one of the men said, but never better than they were enjoying on this particular trip. Grant didn't get excited about the deer or duck hunting, but he leaned forward, listening intently, when they started to discuss the fish they had been catching.

"That's what Danny and I are going to do in the morning," he said.

"You'll catch plenty of fish," Keeler said confidently. "The only trouble is that it ruins you for fishing anywhere else."

With that, Keeler and his friends excused themselves and went back to their cabin. When they were gone, Carl Orlis suggested that the rest go into the living room for their evening devotions.

"What's that?" Grant whispered to Danny.

"We always have Bible reading and prayer in the evening. Don't you?"

His cousin laughed. "You wouldn't ask that if you knew my dad. He won't even go to church—except at Easter and Christmas."

"That's too bad," Danny said.

"I don't know. He seems to get by okay."

Before Danny had a chance to say more, his cousin hurried into the living room where he took a chair as far from Carl Orlis as possible.

The following day, Danny and Grant were up before six o'clock. The sun was already high above the trees on the east bank of the creek, warming the faint breeze that was teasing the placid waters of the bay. Danny stepped out of the little cabin and looked about. The front door of his parents' house was open, indicating that they were already up, and his mom was probably busy cooking breakfast. Cap and Jim were at the stern of the *Island Queen*, making space for the luggage of tourists who would be boarding at Oak and Flag Islands.

Grant joined Danny. "Think we had any visitors last night?"

Danny frowned. "It doesn't look that way from here, but we don't know about the buildings at the back. Somebody could have broken into them."

Grant started toward the shed where they had stored the outboard motors. Young Orlis caught up with him, and they hurried up the slight slope together.

Although they would not have been surprised had the shed been broken into, the lock was still in place, and there was no sign that it had been tampered with.

"It looks as though everything's all right," Danny said in relief. "We can be thankful for that."

Grant glanced quizzically at his cousin, as though he was surprised at the last remark—but he said nothing.

The boys unlocked the shed, got out the motors that would be used that day, mounted them onto the boats, and filled the gas tanks. They knew the fishermen would be wanting to go out on the lake right after breakfast, and they didn't want to keep them waiting.

Shortly after Keeler and his friends pulled away from the Orlis dock, the two boys got their gear and set off in the *Scappoose*, Danny's boat. They headed into the bay and angled in the direction of Little McCoy Island.

"Think the fish'll be biting over this way?" Grant asked.

"We'll soon find out," Danny told him.

The lake was calm, and the little boat sped over the placid surface, leaving a wake that curved outward from the boat in an ever-widening vee. They had almost reached the island when Grant caught a glimpse of a small craft a mile or so away.

"Looks like we're going to have company," he said.

Danny slowed the *Scappoose*, and, shading his eyes with a bronzed hand, stared in the direction his companion pointed.

"That's got to be a canoe," he said.

"Are you sure?"

"Positive. And from the speed its traveling, it's powered by a small outboard."

"So?"

"Hardly anybody lives in that direction," Danny continued. "And no one over there even owns a canoe, let alone uses one on the bay." He reached for the handle of his motor. "I think we'd better go over there and have a look, so we'll know who it is."

His cousin drew in his breath sharply. "Are you sure it isn't the thief?"

Danny grinned. "No one could be real sure about that. But I can say this much, I don't think it is."

"How come?"

"Would you be out on the lake running around in a conspicuous rig like that guy is using if you were stealing stuff in the area?"

Grant did not answer him.

"No way," young Orlis repeated. "He'd be keeping out of sight so nobody would get suspicious."

With that, Danny twisted the handle on his outboard. The *Scappoose* leaped forward, the bow lifting high momentarily. As the little boat picked up speed and came up on plane, the bow dropped noticeably.

At first the stranger in the canoe didn't notice them. When he did, he turned the light craft hurriedly and headed for the nearest islands.

CHAPTER 2

THE ILL-TEMPERED TOM LEFEVRE

Danny turned the handle of the outboard as far as he could, endeavoring to coax even more speed from the laboring motor—but it was useless. The *Scappoose* was racing over the calm surface with the drone of ten thousand bees. It was closing the gap between itself and the canoe rapidly, but the lighter craft was too far ahead. By the time Danny and Grant reached the islands, the canoe was not to be seen.

"What do you suppose happened to him?" Grant asked, staring curiously about.

Danny frowned. "I don't have a clue."

Disappointment lined his cousin's lean features. "What do we do now? Nose around looking for him?"

"We can," Danny said, "but it's not going to do much good. He could pull that canoe up into the brush, and we'd never see it—unless we happened to go ashore at exactly the right place."

Grant stood and stared intently about—first in one direction and then in another. "I'd sure like to get a look at him," he said.

"Me too." Danny swung the *Scappoose* parallel to the nearest finger of rocks and forest that thrust proudly out of the water. For several minutes he crept along one island after another. They eyed the shoreline tautly but could see nothing out of the ordinary. No telltale marks in the sand indicated the spot where the canoe had been pulled up on the beach, and no flash of color in the bush revealed its hiding place. It was almost as though the canoe and its sole occupant had been swept from that end of the Lake of the Woods.

"Are you sure we saw something?" Grant asked finally.

"I don't know about you," Danny said grinning, "but I know *I* did. I'd stake my life on it."

"I–I guess I would, too," Grant said uncertainly. "But, whoever he was, he disappeared so fast it made me wonder for a minute or two...." He paused significantly. "What do you suppose happened to him, anyway?"

Danny Orlis shrugged. "He's around here some-where, but if he lies low, I don't think we'll see any more of him on this trip."

With that, he slowed the *Scappoose* to trolling speed, and they got out their rods and reels, playing out line slowly to allow their lures to trail some distance behind the boat. For an hour or more, they fished in comparative silence. Grant caught two undersized walleyes that he released carefully, and Danny got a northern large enough to furnish them with meat for their shore lunch.

While they trolled, the boys studied the shoreline carefully, trying to find some clue that would indicate where the man in the canoe had gone ashore. But they found nothing. The sandy beach was packed firm and smooth by the action of the waves, and there were no freshly broken branches on the tangle of brush and trees that covered the island.

"Still no sign of that dude," Danny said.

Grant laughed. "Maybe he came in a UFO and took off for outer space."

"That's about as good an explanation of what happened as I've been able to come up with." His frown deepened. "That guy's *got* to be around here some place close. We were gaining on him when he went around the corner of that island and 'pouf'—he disappeared."

An hour later, Danny nosed the *Scappoose* into a sandy beach, and they got out to fix a shore lunch. Grant gathered dry sticks from the dead lower branches of nearby trees while Danny filleted the fish. Using a sharp knife that he kept in his tackle box for that purpose, he slit the pike's belly, cut down to the backbone just behind the gills, and, turning his knife, sliced a thick slab of meat off each side. He cleaned the fish so expertly that there was little flesh left along the bones. Then he removed the skin and the rib bones from each fillet.

By the time he was ready to fry the fish, his cousin had the fire ready. He stripped the label from a can of beans, removed the top, and set the can in one corner of the flames.

"Man!" Grant exclaimed, tasting the food. "This is the best fish I've ever eaten!"

"It does taste good out in the open like this."

"You can say that again. It's too bad that guy in the canoe isn't around close. If he smelled this fish, he'd be here pronto trying to bum something to eat."

They finished the last of the pike, put the can and paper plates in a plastic bag they had brought along for that purpose, and covered the remnants of the fire with wet sand. Only then were they ready to go out on the water again.

Danny and Grant fished three hours that afternoon, catching close to their limit, before heading back home. Keeler and his friends were still on the lake, but by the time the boys had their fish cleaned, the other fishermen had come in with tales of a jet boat they had seen.

"I don't know of anyone on the Angle who's got a jet," Danny said.

"We don't know who he is," one of the Keeler party put in, "but there's a jet boat here now. It's the only thing that would go so fast on the water. 'Whoosh'—and it was gone! Left us like we were standing still." He paused significantly. "He headed the direction you said you were going. Are you positive you didn't see him?"

Danny shook his head. "All we saw was a guy in a red canoe."

"That was probably the same guy. His boat was red too."

"The rig we saw wasn't high enough to be a boat," Danny protested, "and it didn't go 'whoosh'—it went 'put-put-put.'"

"We were close enough to get a good look at him," the fisherman went on. "At his boat, I mean. It didn't look very big when it wasn't under power. I don't think it had more than six inches of freeboard."

"But a jet makes a lot of racket," young Orlis protested. "The rig we saw didn't make any that we could hear."

"Of course," Grant said, "it was going slow."

"Anyway," Keeler put in, "the guy was sure acting strange. I thought he was going to challenge us to a race, but he didn't. He kept right on going."

The next morning, as soon as Danny and Grant had finished their chores for the day, they went out onto the lake once more. They had their gear in the boat and were about to shove off when Mrs. Orlis came to the door and called to Danny.

"Hang in there, Grant," Danny said. "I'll go see what Mom wants."

He was back a moment later, scowling.

"Something wrong?" his cousin asked as he stepped into the boat and pushed away from the dock.

"She wants us to stop by Tom LeFevre's place and see if he's all right. He came over a couple of weeks ago and asked Dad to get some things from town for him, but he hasn't been back to pick them up. She's afraid he's sick or something."

"That doesn't sound like such a big deal. What's so bad about it?"

"You don't know him, or you wouldn't say that. He's an ugly-tempered old man who lives on the Canadian side. He's chased me away from his place more than once. Wouldn't even loan me enough gas to get home when I ran out one time. I had to row all the way."

Grant was silent momentarily. "Why would your mom care about such an angry old man as that?"

"She's that way about everybody. If someone is sick, Mom's over there to help in any way she can." Danny turned out of Pine Creek and headed across the bay. "She says that Christ helped those who were in need—and it's the least she can do."

"I can understand helping someone who's nice and agreeable, but a guy like that! It doesn't make sense!"

"It does to her."

His cousin thought about that for a time. "I'll tell you what. I'll stay in the boat. *You* can go up and see how he is."

"No way! If I'm in trouble, you're in trouble! And don't you forget it!"

Danny didn't go directly to LeFevre's place. Since it was on the Canadian side, he detoured to the Canadian Customs Office on an island near the mouth of the bay. The officer on duty came to the door as he heard the approach of the *Scappoose*. When he saw it was Danny and his cousin, he waved and motioned them on. He knew the boys would not be going far.

As they neared Smuggler's Point, Danny saw a thin spiral of smoke twisting up into the cloudless, blue sky.

"LeFevre must be all right," he said. "There's smoke coming out of his chimney."

"I'm glad that's settled," Grant told him. "Now we won't have to go ashore."

"Oh yes, we will. That's not going to be good enough for Mom. She said she wanted us to *see* Tom LeFevre—and that's what we've got to do, or we'll be in real trouble when we get home."

They skirted a long, narrow island and turned toward the clearing on the mainland behind it. Someone was there. That would have been obvious, even if there had been no fire in the kitchen stove. A cumbersome, flat-bottomed commercial fishing boat was tied along the dock, and a canoe was pulled out of the water and turned upside down.

The cabin door was open, and a skinny, rib-showing dog chased a small squirrel across the yard.

As Danny and Grant turned toward the dock, a boy about their own age came out of the cabin and sauntered to the wooden platform that extended out into the lake. He was almost as tall as Danny but was slight of build—a string bean with arms and legs, a surly smirk disfiguring his gaunt features.

"Hi!" Danny called out.

The boy on shore only grunted and made no move to reach for the line Grant tried to hand him. Nor did he move out of the way when Danny's cousin stepped onto the dock. Grant collided with him, and they both came close to falling in.

"What'd you do that for?" the young stranger demanded.

"I'm sorry."

"You *ought* to be."

When the *Scappoose* was secured and Danny was on the dock, the boy turned to him. "What do you want?" he snarled.

"Mom was worried about Mr. LeFevre," Danny replied, keeping his voice steady. "He asked Dad to get some things for him in town, and he hasn't been over to pick them up. That was two weeks ago. She thought maybe he had been sick or hurt."

"That old buzzard?" the young stranger echoed. "He's too mean to have anything happen to him."

"You sound as though you know him pretty well," Danny said. He didn't think much of the boy's attitude, but he had to admit that he agreed with his appraisal of the old man.

"I ought to. He's my mom's dad."

"And you're here visiting?"

"I *hope!* Though Mum says we might be living here quite a while. My old man run off and left us, and we didn't have anywhere else to go."

"That's too bad."

"You can say that again! I'd go out of my mind if I had to live here all the time." He lowered his voice. "You'd never believe how that old man treats me! Every time I turn around, he's yelling about something I've done or didn't do. Two or three times he's beaten me half to death!"

At that instant, a lean figure appeared in the doorway.

"Stephen!" a hostile voice rasped. "How many times have I told you that we don't want strangers around here? Tell those two to get on their way, and you come back to the house before I belt you good!"

Danny Orlis started forward hesitantly. He didn't like the thought of having to face LeFevre again, but he couldn't allow the old man's grandson to take the blame for their visit.

"It's me. Danny Orlis!" he stammered. "And it's not Steve's fault that we're here. Mom sent us over to see how you're doing. She's been worried about you."

The old man's manner softened slightly—but only for a moment.

"That's a likely story. Now get back in that boat of yours and head out! We've got trouble enough around here as it is! We don't need your kind!"

"I'm telling you the truth," Danny persisted. "You were at our place and asked Dad to order some things from Warroad for you. We haven't seen you since. Mom thought you may not have come because you were sick or had been hurt, so she asked us to come by and see if you're all right."

"I was planning to come and get that stuff one of these days." He drew himself tall. "Tell your dad he doesn't need to worry about getting the money he put out. If he is, he can use the stuff or take it back, and I'll get into town on my own and buy it. Probably should have done that anyway. That dad of yours makes money on me every time I have him buy something. Charges me more than he has to pay!"

Danny bristled. "You know better than that!"

"I know he says he doesn't," LeFevre countered belligerently, "but that doesn't mean he hasn't been lying to me."

"You've lived around my dad for a long time, Mr. LeFevre! You ought to know by this time that he doesn't lie, and he doesn't cheat! Ask anybody! They'll tell you!"

CHAPTER 3

THE MAN IN THE BUSH

The ill-tempered Indian glared at Danny and Grant, then at his grandson, as though he still held him responsible for the appearance of the youthful intruders.

"Get back to the garden like your mom told you to an hour ago!" he snarled. "You've got to do *something* around here to earn your keep!"

Anger twisted the boy's face. "Shut up, you old goat! I do as I please!"

LeFevre snatched a stick and brandished it menacingly in Steve's direction. "Do as I say!" he bellowed, "or I'll break this on your back!"

His grandson retreated warily. As he did so, he put his thumbs in his ears and waggled them derisively. "You've got to catch me first!" With that he fled into the bush behind him.

LeFevre recoiled as though he had been slapped, and the strength seemed to leave his body.

"Rachel!" he shouted over his shoulder. "Come here!"

A moment later, a spindling, black-haired woman who bore the same harsh features as her dad appeared in the doorway. She was probably several years younger than Danny's mom, but she looked to be much older.

"What do you want now?" she snapped.

"You've got to do something about that brat of yours. He won't do a thing I tell 'im to!"

Helplessness flecked her brown eyes. "If you want something done about Stephen, do it yourself! You know he don't pay no attention to anything *I* say!"

"I'll do something, all right! I'll knock his head off!" Then he remembered that Danny and Grant were still standing there. He turned to them. "Tell that dad of yours I'll be over in a day or two—okay?"

The boys started for the *Scappoose*, and LeFevre followed them.

"Had any trouble around your place lately?" he asked as they loosed the boat and got into it.

"Trouble?" Danny echoed.

"Yeah. Thieves!" His eyes narrowed. "You've heard about it, haven't you?"

Young Orlis nodded. "Mr. Sherwood was over our way a couple of days ago telling Dad that he had lost some things."

"I've been figuring I'm next," LeFevre continued, suspicion gleaming in his dark features. "I'm a neighbor to Sherwood. It isn't likely that they'd hit him and let me off free. But I've got my rifle handy. Anybody who tries to steal from me is in for a big surprise."

The boys shoved the *Scappoose* away from the dock and started the motor.

"Did you hear what he said just now?" Grant asked, when they were some distance from the little clearing.

"How could I miss it? That character acted like he suspects *us* of stealing those things at Sherwood's."

"I know. I wanted to tell him he could forget that. We hadn't done it."

"It wouldn't have done any good. Trying to tell him anything would make him more suspicious than ever."

Back on shore, Tom LeFevre returned to the house and got his rifle. "If that kid of yours comes home before I do," he stormed, "get him out on that garden! If he stays around here, he's got to earn his keep!"

His daughter glared angrily but said nothing.

"You hear me?" he snarled.

"Yes, I heard you!"

"Just put him to work! That's all I ask!"

With that, he stormed out of the house and up the path toward the edge of the clearing. He paused at the line of poplar and jack pine that ringed his little plot of land and looked about intently.

That Orlis kid and his friend could be guilty, he told himself. The boys could have made up that story about Mrs. Orlis wanting them to stop and see how he was doing. Why would *she* care anything about him and whether he was sick or hurt? Most of the white people he knew wouldn't care what happened to an Indian man—especially someone like himself.

He had to admit he had never heard anything bad about Danny or his parents. Everybody liked them—in spite of the fact that they were so religious. He knew what Ivar Sherwood or any of the other neighbors would say if he mentioned suspecting that Orlis kid and his friend. The boy did have a good reputation, but maybe that was just a dodge—part of the act to keep anyone from looking his direction for the thief.

Anyway, it didn't hurt to put Danny and the other kid on guard—just in case. If they were guilty, they might be afraid to hit his place, knowing he was already suspicious of them.

LeFevre heard the mournful call of a loon that drifted to him on the still morning air. He remained motionless until it died away. Then he started forward, circling the clearing with diligence.

He was an experienced hunter and knew the woods as well as most men knew their own backyards. He read the game trails skillfully, noting the broken branches, the bent ferns, and the new indentations in the moss that indicated a moose had gone by. Here a doe and twin fawns had bedded down for the night after feeding on the spindling willow and pin cherry trees that grew along the low places. A bit farther, a timber wolf had caught a snowshoe rabbit and had his dinner beneath a clump of birch.

LeFevre made his way up a small hill overlooking his clearing and the bay when he stopped suddenly, his senses alert. The moss and ferns were trampled, and half a dozen cigarette butts were scattered about, along with a number of match sticks.

He picked up one of the matches and studied it carefully. It was of the kitchen variety and had been broken in two. A few men cultivated that habit when they struck a match in the bush, in order to give the flame a little more time to go out before dropping it to the ground, where it might start a fire.

He frowned thoughtfully. Not long ago he had seen someone do that—someone he knew well—but he couldn't remember who it was. The incident nagged at him as he turned back to his examination.

Whoever was spying on his place had left a short time before. The broken ferns had not yet begun to brown, and the faint smell of cigarette smoke still lingered in the air.

LeFevre sat down on the log the other man had used and parted the brush slightly. He could look down on his house, the smaller buildings, and the clear, calm water beyond. The man who chose the spot had chosen it well. He could observe everything that went on without being seen himself.

An honest man wouldn't come up to a spot like this, the tall Indian decided. A man with honorable intentions would not sneak through the brush and remain hidden. He would come boldly into the yard, knock on the door, and state his business.

LeFevre remained motionless for a time, staring into the brush around him, searching for some sign that the one who had been there earlier was still nearby watching all that went on. Then, satisfied that the stranger had fled, he set out, following the trail that had been left.

The stranger knew the woods, that was certain. He had made his way unerringly along the ridge. After a mile or so, he turned off and followed a game trail down the gentle slope. At the bottom, he skirted a finger of muskeg that reached out from a narrow stream winding through the bush.

LeFevre had been tracking the stranger for half an hour or more when he stopped and pulled himself up. Only one family lived in this direction, and the trail he was following led straight for that place.

His pulse quickened.

Ivar Sherwood!

And he was the one who always broke his matches before throwing them down! Sweat glistened on the old Indian's forehead. Ivar couldn't be the thief! They had been neighbors for years. They had traded work with each other and had even trapped together for two seasons. And that time when he had been sick, his neighbor had come over and worked his nets.

That time when Sherwood's wife was sick and the doctors couldn't seem to help, Tom LeFevre had gone out in the bush for certain roots that would help a bad heart. She got better almost immediately and lived for three more years. Sherwood had always been grateful.

No, his friend wouldn't steal from him! Anybody else on the Angle, perhaps, but not him! He paused significantly, the corners of his mouth tightening. Or would he? Now that he thought about it, Ivar had acted strange the last time he stopped by. He acted nervous as a jaybird and wouldn't even come in for a cup of tea. All he wanted to do was talk about the thievery.

Sherwood talked a lot about his things that had been stolen, but maybe that was only a dodge. Maybe he hadn't had anything stolen. Maybe he just talked about it to everyone so nobody would suspect him when they began to miss things.

Now that he thought about it, his friend had had a poor trapping season the year before, and so far, his commercial fishing hadn't gone much better. The last time LeFevre had been in Kenora, the manager at the Bay Store asked about Sherwood. Said they were going to have to quit giving him credit until he paid something on his bill. When the Indian looked at it that way, things did add up.

He straightened slowly, the lines about his mouth deepening. The evidence pointed suspiciously toward his neighbor—there was no denying that. On the other hand, he had to be sure before he said any-thing. How could such a thing be true? Sherwood had a reputation for being as honest as Carl Orlis.

In all the years Ivar and his family had lived on the Angle, no one had ever found anything in the man's character to criticize. Even in the face of such damaging facts as those LeFevre just uncovered, he doubted that his neighbor would take anything that didn't belong to him.

He would watch Ivar Sherwood closely, he decided. Only a fool would ignore the warning signs he had seen. But he wasn't saying anything to anyone just yet. There was plenty of time for that to come later—after he knew for sure. He shifted his rifle to his right hand and made his way up the point in the direction of his own cabin.

* * * *

Danny and Grant fished among the islands for several hours, catching several walleyes and northerns apiece. Finally they noted the time and headed in the direction of Pine Creek and home. By the time they got back to the Orlis place and had their fish cleaned, it would be time for supper.

"I'm sure glad I don't have to live with a guy like that Tom LeFevre," Grant said. "That would be awful!"

Danny nodded. He had been punished by his parents for things he had done that he shouldn't and probably would be again. They saw to it that he did what he was told. But they had never talked to him like old Tom LeFevre had talked to his grandson. It made Danny appreciate his parents all the more.

"That Steve is no prize package," Danny's cousin continued, "but I sure don't blame him for the way he acted. I'd probably do the same if I was abused like that."

Danny could understand why his cousin felt the way he did, but it wasn't the way the Bible said kids were to act. His disapproval must have been written in his features.

"Do you?" Grant asked.

"Do I *what?*" Danny countered.

"Blame Steve for being like he is—so angry and disagreeable, I mean."

Young Orlis hesitated. "My parents sure don't treat me that way, and I don't think your dad gives you a hard time, either. But we don't treat them the way Steve treats his granddad. I don't know *what* my dad would do to me if I called him an old goat! He wouldn't beat me, but I'd sure know better than to do it again."

Grant frowned, as though he wasn't sure he agreed with Danny.

"Parents and grandparents aren't supposed to abuse their kids," young Orlis went on, "but the Bible says we're supposed to obey those who are in authority over us. I think that means we ought to treat them with respect, too."

"Even a guy like his grandfather?"

"Even a guy like Steve's grandfather."

"That's awful! It sure doesn't make sense to me! I couldn't take it. I'd run away. *Nobody* ought to have to take that kind of stuff!"

Danny didn't argue with his cousin. In fact, he found it difficult not to feel the same way. He knew his dad would not approve of the way LeFevre screamed at Steve and threatened him. But he had the uneasy feeling that his dad would also say that the boy should do a lot more than he was doing in an effort to get along with his vile-tempered old grandfather.

They were drawing close to the final opening between the islands that led to the open water of the bay when he heard the sudden roar of a powerful motor. Almost at the same time Grant shouted to him and pointed. Danny turned quickly—in time to see a speedboat bearing down on them. The gap between the two boats was closing rapidly.

Danny caught his breath! The speedboat was headed straight for them, giving no indication of turning! The taunting grin of the young driver infuriated him as he shoved the motor desperately to one side in a wild attempt to avoid the racing craft! A prayer caught in his throat as the *Scappoose* responded sluggishly.

CHAPTER 4

DANNY TO THE RESCUE

The *Scappoose* had been going at a fast clip moments before. Now it seemed to crawl as it struggled to come about and avoid collision with the roaring jet. Danny twisted the throttle even harder than before, but the motor was already wide open. A scream formed on Grant's lips, but no sound came out. He stared wildly at the boy behind the wheel of the other boat and clung to the seat with both hands.

Momentarily the grin lingered on the jet driver's face as he heaved hard on the wheel—but nothing happened. The grin gave way to terror as he lunged again at the controls. For an instant, the speeding craft seemed locked on course, headed for destruction. Then it changed directions slightly. Not much—just enough away from the *Scappoose* to squeeze by. The slower rig shuddered as the gunnel of the speedboat nicked her bow.

An instant later, the surging wake slammed into the *Scappoose,* and she shipped water. But Danny and Grant scarcely noticed. They were staring in horror as the jet raced toward the island. The driver was still fighting the wheel, but something had gone wrong and it wouldn't budge. He reached for the throttle, jerking it back as though it, too, was stuck.

Only it wasn't. The fast-moving boat lunged to a halt so suddenly that the boy at the wheel was caught off guard. He sailed forward, over the windshield. His slight form spread-eagled, and he slammed into the water a hundred yards or so offshore. The wake surged over the stern of the jet, half filling the cockpit with water.

Danny brought the *Scappoose* about and raced toward the boy lying face down on the placid surface.

"He's knocked out!" Grant cried.

"Take over!" Danny shouted, bringing his boat to a halt nearby. With that, he dove in and swam over to the inert figure. Grasping the lad by the hair, he turned him over and pulled him to the *Scappoose* with powerful strokes.

"Now what do you want me to do?" Grant demanded as Danny grasped the side of his boat.

"Start the engine and take us close enough to shore so I can reach the bottom. And watch out for the rocks!"

Danny clung to the smaller boat with one hand and the victim of the strange accident with the other until his feet touched the bottom. Then, hurriedly, he pulled the young stranger to the beach, where he gave him CPR. Grant nosed the *Scappoose* ashore, jumped out, and joined his cousin.

"Is–Is he–" He dared not even voice the fears that troubled him.

Prayerfully Danny worked. He had been taught three years earlier how to revive a drowning person. His dad had seen to that. But this was the first time he had ever been forced to use what he had learned.

He worked slowly, rhythmically, trying to get the boy started breathing again. Grant knelt close by, his own breath short and rasping. He stared intently at the scene before him. He wanted to speak—to ask Danny if there was any sign of life—but he could not. All he could do was wait.

For several minutes the boy lay motionless, then he coughed and began to breathe. At first his breath came in thin, shallow gasps. Then he moved his legs slightly and groaned between clenched teeth. He opened his eyes and closed them again, but in a few minutes he was breathing almost normally.

Danny straightened, tears of thankfulness in his eyes.

"He's going to be all right!" Grant murmured. He, too, was shaken by the incident. "He's going to be all right!"

"Thank You, God!" Danny prayed aloud. "Thank You!"

For several minutes, the older boy lay on the beach with his eyes closed. Finally, however, he rolled on his side and raised himself on one elbow. He was still badly unnerved. His cheeks were ashen, and his lips trembled uncontrollably.

"W-What happened?" he demanded, looking from Danny to Grant and back again.

"Your steering gear must have jammed," young Orlis told him. "You almost rammed us, and when you jerked back on the throttle, your boat stopped so quickly that you were thrown out." He paused. "You had a close call."

The older lad brushed a hand across his features in a nervous gesture. "You can say that again."

"Feel okay now?"

He shook his head. "To tell you the truth, I–I don't know. The last I remember, I was flying through the air."

"You did that, all right," Danny said. "You looked like a pelican coming in to land."

The other boy ignored his remark. "Did you pull me out of the water?"

"We were right there when it happened. It was no big deal."

"It was to me! I'd have drowned if you hadn't gotten me out and worked on me until I started breathing again." He paused, and when he spoke again, he changed the subject abruptly. "I can swim, but I must've been knocked out. I don't remember a thing from the time I went flying through the air until a couple of minutes ago."

"You're all right now," Danny said. "That's the main thing."

The three boys sat on shore for half an hour or more, doing very little talking. After a time, the stranger introduced himself. His name was Peter Starr, he said. He was seventeen years old and was spending the summer with his mom at their place on the Canadian side of the big lake. His dad had a law office in Winnipeg and came out for weekends.

Danny knew the name well. Everybody on the lake talked about the size and splendor of the Starr home that had been built three years before. There were other nice houses scattered along the vast lakeshore, but none to compare to the Starr place. He had never been ashore but had gone by it several times, both in the *Scappoose* and in Cap's *Island Queen*. It was the biggest house he had ever seen.

There had to be at least six bedrooms and, judging by the number of chimneys, at least that many fireplaces. It had been built of factory-shaped logs, with a stone foundation and huge triple-glass windows to keep out the cold.

There were several fairly large buildings on the clearing. One housed a generator to furnish electricity. Another provided space for their boats and snowmobiles to be kept out of the weather. The third was a workshop. According to Danny's dad, it was as well-equipped as one would find in most towns the size of Kenora. Anything that might be needed around such a place was there.

Peter got to his feet and walked up and down the beach. His first steps were short and uncertain, but gradually he was able to move out with a firm, sure stride.

"You're coming along great," Danny said.

"Yeah." He came back and sat on the bow of the *Scappoose.* "Only I've still got a problem. I've got a boat out there that's half-filled with water, and I can't steer it. Not only that, but I'm eight miles from home."

"Not a problem," Danny said. "It's early. We'll help you bail out the water and tow you back to your place."

"We'll take care of the water easier than that," Peter said. "I've got an electric bilge pump on the old tub. I can turn that on, and we'll be rid of the water in ten minutes."

"Sounds good," Danny replied. "Hop in, and we'll go out and get started."

They reached the jet boat in a moment or two. It had taken on so much water that the gunnels were almost awash. Peter leaned over the side and switched on the pump. Immediately, water began to squirt from a plastic-lined hole at the stern.

"We could leave the boat here," the older boy said, reluctance creeping into his voice even as he spoke. "Saunders could come and get it. The old man keeps him around for jobs we don't want to do, but I'd get a lot of grief if Dad finds out. He's on my case all the time as it is."

"Like I said," Danny continued, "it's not that much of a problem. We can tow you to your place in a couple of hours."

Peter reached for his wallet. "I'll give you a hundred bucks if you will," he said, fishing the money from his wallet. "It's worth that much to me to keep the old man off my case."

"Put your money away," Danny told him. "Up here we all try to help each other as much as we can, and we don't expect to be paid for it."

Peter shrugged indifferently. "Suit yourself. But I think you're stupid not to take the money while you've got the chance."

When the bilge pump had done its work, Danny used his anchor rope to pull the jet boat with the *Scappoose*. They started slowly and picked up speed until they were moving about five miles an hour. It seemed as though they were crawling, but any greater speed caused the jet to fishtail, jerking the *Scappoose* to one side and then the other. Grant and Peter almost fell asleep—but Danny had to keep wide awake. It was up to him to maintain a close watch for rocks as they picked their way among the islands in the direction of the Starr home.

He noticed that Peter had begun to fidget nervously toward the end of the long, tedious trip. He obviously had something on his mind, but it was not until the Starr summer home was in sight that he spoke.

"What do you figure on telling your old man about what happened today?" he asked suddenly.

Danny's gaze met his and held there. "I haven't thought much about what I'll tell my parents. Why?"

"You don't have to tell 'em nothin', do you?"

"I don't suppose I do—but I usually let them know what happened when I've been out on the lake. The important things, anyway."

Peter hesitated. "You can keep your trap shut this time! It won't hurt you!"

"Why should I keep quiet?" Danny asked him.

"Last week I–I came a little close to another boat," he stammered. "It was nothing dangerous. I was just giving them a thrill the way I did you guys. Anyway, one of those dudes knew my dad. He squealed on me, and you should have heard the old man! Stormed around like I'd half killed somebody. He warned me not to do it again. Said if he heard about anything like that again I'd be grounded for a whole month! Wouldn't be able to go out in my boat or go fishing or anything!"

"If my parents ask me how you came to have trouble with your boat, I'll tell them," Danny replied evenly.

"It wouldn't hurt you to tell a little white lie. You could say that we were racing and my steering jammed. That's *almost* the truth."

"Almost isn't good enough," Danny answered. "My dad would never buy that story. You've got to be out of your mind if you think he'd believe I would even *try* to race a jet boat with the *Scappoose*."

"Then you think of something."

"No way. I don't lie—especially to my parents, whether I could make them believe it or not."

Anger flecked the other boy's eyes, and the corners of his mouth drooped petulantly. "It wouldn't *hurt* you any."

Danny looked back to check their tow without answering.

"Would it?" Peter repeated.

"More than you could know."

"But they'd never find out. I swear!" He pulled out his wallet again and held it in his hand. "I don't suppose there's any way I can get you to change your mind."

Danny shook his head.

Peter swore. "I don't know why you're so stubborn. They'd never find out. I guarantee it!"

"Even if no one *else* ever found out, I'd know. There's no use arguing about it, Peter. I'm not going out of the way to tell what happened, but if my parents want to know, they're going to get the truth. That's all there is to it!"

"I've heard you were so all-fired religious that you never have any fun, but I didn't believe it until now!"

Danny Orlis grinned. "I'm a Christian," he said, "if that's what you mean. And I try hard to live the way God says we should, but I have my share of fun, too."

Peter snorted indignantly. "I'll bet!"

Danny did not answer him. There was no use in saying more. Peter's mind was already made up. Talk would fall on deaf ears.

Saunders, the handyman who worked around the Starr place, came down to the dock and helped them untie Peter's boat and get it into the lift so it could be hoisted above the force of the waves.

"Looks like ye had a bit of trouble, Laddie," the gray-haired man said.

"The steering stuck," Peter lied. "That's all."

Saunders laughed shortly. "Aye," he said, a trace of scorn edging his voice. "Aye, that is what ye say, but do ye always go swimming with your clothes on?"

Peter's cheeks flushed, and he turned to Danny and Grant. "Thanks for the tow," he said. "I'll see you around again as soon as I get this old scow in working order."

CHAPTER 5

HAS SOMEBODY GOT IT IN FOR YOU?

Tom LeFevre made his way to the dock and for several minutes stared uneasily across the shimmering water. A pair of pelicans, looming large as boats on the still surface, fished for their breakfast. A bald eagle wheeled against the pale blue sky, his wings motionless. The sun was high over the eastern reaches of the Lake of the Woods, and it was time for him to go out and lift his nets once more. Past time. But he didn't feel like it. He was going to have to make up his mind about Ivar Sherwood. If he didn't take some sort of action soon, he would be hit by that thief. Then it would be too late.

He couldn't afford to lose even so much as a can of gas or a few shells for his rifle. It was difficult enough to earn a living for himself. Now he had his daughter and that ungrateful son of hers to look after. He couldn't make it and have a sneak thief help himself to his pitifully few belongings.

Why couldn't the trail he followed have led to some other settler? Anyone at all. He could storm up to most any home on the lake and accuse the man of plotting to steal from him. If the guy was guilty, he would soon find out that he'd better leave Tom LeFevre alone. He was onto him. If the guy wasn't guilty and lost his temper, so be it. The gain would be worth the risk. At least he wouldn't be standing by helplessly while some character planned to rob him blind.

But it wasn't anyone else on the lake. It was Ivar Sherwood. He picked up a stick and broke it in two with his gnarled hands. How could he go to a friend—the only real friend he ever had—and tell him he knew he was out to steal from him?

LeFevre was still rolling that question over in his mind when he lifted his nets and brought the fish in and iced them for shipping down to Warroad on the *Bert Steel* or the *Island Queen*. But as things worked out, he didn't have to be concerned about that. He was on his way from the icehouse to the shed where he kept his gas barrels when a familiar boat pulled up at his dock, and a hoarse voice hailed him.

"Tom! I'm glad you're home!" Sherwood threw a double half hitch around the cleat, secured his boat, and stepped up on the dock. "I'm glad I was able to catch you," the bluff, good-natured neighbor repeated.

"Thought maybe you were traipsing about the lake, and I wouldn't find you this morning."

"Just got back," he muttered. Somehow he felt uneasy talking to Ivar after all the dark thoughts he had been harboring about him. "How about a coffee?"

"Sounds good, but I'd like to talk to you a minute first." He lowered his voice. "Don't want to scare your daughter and her kid."

Tom nodded indifferently and led Ivar to one side, away from the house. As he did so, he saw Stephen in the doorway, eyeing him curiously. If that kid got half a chance, he'd be trying to sneak close enough to find out what was going on. It probably didn't make all that much difference. Ivar couldn't have any life-or-death secrets to divulge, but he didn't like it, anyway. When it came right down to it, there wasn't much he liked about Stephen, even if he was his grandson.

"What's up, Ivar?" he asked.

"I wasn't going to tell you this, but I figured you need to know so you can be on the lookout," his friend continued. "I was out hunting back of your place a few days ago. Thought I might come across that coyote that's been getting my chickens. I saw somebody sneaking through the woods not far from your place—and he wasn't wanting to be seen!"

LeFevre drew himself up, his eyes narrowing suspiciously. A likely story, that one, he thought, wondering whether Ivar Sherwood actually expected him to believe it.

"Go on."

"He acted so secret-like that I thought maybe he was watching your place, trying to find out where you had things stashed so he could break in over here like he did at my place."

The slender Indian nodded. "I've been thinking about that myself."

"You have?" Sherwood exclaimed. "Then you've seen him?"

"I saw where somebody had been spying on us. I've been trying to decide what to do about it."

"That was me!" his friend continued. "But that's what I want to talk to you about. After I saw him, I came over here two or three times to keep an eye on things. Thought maybe I might be able to catch him—or at least get a line on who he is. But he didn't show up, as far as I know."

LeFevre's features hardened. "Is that what you came to tell me?"

Sherwood shook his head. "Part of it. I figure I might've spooked the guy. I tried to be as careful as I could, but he could have found out I was there and guessed the reason. If he did, that would be enough to make him lay off for a while."

"Are you saying I got no need to worry?" In spite of himself, ice edged his voice.

"Oh, no. Nothing like that. I wanted to warn you to keep a closer watch than ever. I ain't going in the woods near you, for a while, anyway. If he thinks the coast is clear, he might get careless and decide to try to rob you."

"So?"

"So you can catch 'im if he does!"

"Sounds like a good idea," LeFevre said tersely.

That seemed to satisfy Ivar Sherwood that he had done what he could to help his friend. "Now," he said, smiling broadly, "how about that coffee?"

They went to the house and sat down at the table. Rachel grumbled about having to cook all day, but she brewed them some coffee and brought out smoked fish and rolls. Sherwood hadn't been over to visit for some time and was eager to talk. He told about his fishing, the prospects for trapping the next winter, and the price of furs.

But LeFevre was scarcely listening. He was trying to piece the whole affair together—to figure out if Sherwood was actually telling the truth or if his friend had happened to see him in the woods and worked out this lie to cover his tracks.

He wanted to believe Ivar but still hadn't made up his mind whether he could or not when his friend said it was time to leave. LeFevre walked down to the boat with him.

"Thanks for coming over."

"That's the least I could do after everything you've done for me," Sherwood told him. With that, he loosed the line and got into his boat. Then he turned back to LeFevre. "Tom, there's something I've got to ask you."

"Go ahead."

"Does anybody have it in for you?"

LeFevre's face went ashen, and his lips trembled. For an instant, he felt so dizzy he was afraid he would pitch forward into the water.

"Not that I know of," he croaked. "Why?"

Sherwood shrugged. "I was just wondering."

Before Tom could question him further, he started his engine and roared away, waving as he turned in the direction of his own place.

LeFevre remained motionless, rooted to the dock. Sherwood knew something! He knew something he wasn't telling. He had to—or he wouldn't have said what he did. In that instant, all thought of the thief and the fact that he could very well be the next one robbed was forgotten. Maybe Sherwood recognized the guy in the woods as an enemy of LeFevre's—an enemy he didn't know he had. Someone who wanted to get back at him for some unknown reason. Someone who might put a hex on him.

If that happened, he'd be in big trouble! A lot worse than having someone steal a little something. He could lose his luck fishing and hunting. His boat could get loose and be ruined on the rocks. Or he could come down sick. The spirits might even help the thief steal everything he owned. There was no limit to what bad things could happen if the guy who was mad at him went to a powerful witch doctor. And old Rabbit Ear on the Reserve had every Indian in the area afraid of him.

"What'd he mean about somebody having it in for you?" Steve asked suddenly.

LeFevre started, and his heart skipped a beat at the sound of the boy's voice. He had sneaked up to hear what was said, and his grandfather was furious.

"Nothin'!" he exploded. "Nothin' at all! Now get back to that garden and get to work, or I'll give you a lickin' you won't forget! And don't you be sneakin' up behind me like that again! You hear?"

Steve grinned impishly at him. "You're scared!" he taunted.

Rage contorted the old man's face, and he swung his open hand at his grandson. But the boy ducked and jerked away. He said no more, but LeFevre knew what he was thinking—and it infuriated him.

"Just for that you can't use the canoe for a week."

"See if I care!"

"It's *my* canoe!"

Steve was still laughing as he went behind the icehouse and out of sight. His grandfather didn't say any more about his weeding the garden, but he hadn't expected him to. That's the way he was. He got mad and stormed around a lot. But that was all there was to it unless he got awful mad. Then a guy had to watch out. He'd grab up the nearest chunk of wood or piece of iron he could find and start swinging.

At first, Steve didn't know what to expect and caught a few of those blows. When he knew more about his grandfather's temper, he learned to keep out of the way when the old man reached the boiling point. Before long he realized that a lot of the threats that were thrown his way were only noisy blustering and carried little danger of being carried out. He discovered exactly how far he could go without triggering a violent response. Taunting his grandfather became a challenge, and he tried to see how angry he could make him without running the risk of being beaten.

This time, however, he sensed that there was no space for manipulation. The concern the old man felt was so great that Steve dare not press him. To do so would be to invite disaster. So he waited until he was sure Tom LeFevre was back in the house; then he filled the small outboard with mixed gas and oil, put it on the canoe, and shoved off. He paddled around the corner of the nearest island so those in the house couldn't hear the engine when it started. Then he was on his way.

His grandfather would miss the canoe after a time and storm about it for a while, but chances were good that he would have cooled off by the time Steve got home. At least that was the way it usually happened. All of that talk about grounding him for a week or a month didn't mean a thing. He never even tried to enforce such threats.

Steve knew it wouldn't do any good for his grandfather to try to punish him that way. His mum would never stand for it. LeFevre might yell at his daughter enough to make her cry, but Steve knew she could handle the old man if she had a mind to. Let her rare back on her heels and give him a blast and he ran for cover like a rabbit with a dog on his trail.

Steve didn't know why he decided to go over to the Orlis place to see Danny and Grant. It was a long way, even if he didn't go around by Customs, which he didn't plan to do. It was against the law to cross the border at any other place, but he knew from experience that the Customs officials didn't leave their stations. So he would take the chance. In a way, he found it exciting to do things he wasn't supposed to do. It made his spine tingle and his heart beat faster. When he got away with something, he felt like he was smarter than anyone else.

An hour and a half later, Steve pulled into Pine Creek in front of the Orlis place. Grant and Danny's dog came down to the dock to meet him.

"Where is everybody?" he asked.

"Danny'll be back before long. He had to guide some fishermen today."

"Too bad I didn't know it." Steve stepped lightly out of the canoe. "You and I could've gone fishing together."

Grant shook his head. "It wouldn't do you any good to go out with me. Danny's the one who knows the lake. All I do is ride along where he decides to go."

"Maybe *you* don't know where the fish are, but *I* do! I found 'em the other day! Got into a school of walleyes like you wouldn't believe! And big? I could hardly get 'em into the net. Lost a bunch just because I didn't have anyone to net for me."

Grant studied the visitor's dark face curiously. "Are you giving it to me straight?"

"It's the truth, Grant. I swear it! If you'll come over, I'll show you the best fishing you ever had in your whole life."

"Just where is this wonderful place?" Grant persisted skeptically.

"I'll have to show you."

By this time, Danny's cousin was getting excited. "When?"

Steve shrugged. If he made a date to go fishing with Danny and Grant and his grandfather was still mad at him, he might have to disappoint them. But he would take a chance on that. He was bored out of his mind at not being in town where he could be with the gang throwing stones through the windows of empty buildings and keying cars on the street.

"When do we go?" Grant repeated.

"Makes me no difference. How about tomorrow?"

"Sounds great!"

"We could meet on that little island just west of where I'm staying. I'll be there by ten o'clock."

"We could stop by for you."

"I'd better meet you out on the island. The old man don't like you and Danny much," he lied. "Swears you're a bad influence on me." He laughed shortly. "We'd better get together somewhere else—like the island."

CHAPTER 6

PETER'S NEW BOAT

Steve left the Orlis place shortly before Danny and his party returned. They were heading into Pine Creek as he was coming out. Danny slowed the *Scappoose* as though he wanted to stop and talk, but the other boy waved and went on. He had been brave enough when he took the canoe after being ordered to leave it alone. Now, however, he had to return home and face his mum and his grandfather.

A new uneasiness gripped him. He didn't think the old man would do more than storm like he always did about his taking the canoe, but there was the possibility that he might blow his cool and start swinging or throwing things. Steve would never forget the time he threw a spade and almost hit him in the leg. If something like that happened again, he might not be lucky enough to get out of the way in time.

The nearer he got to the Canadian side, the more tense he became. Usually he could come up with some plausible story about where he had been and what he had been doing that would at least sound like the truth. This time, however, he had boxed himself in. Nothing he could say would make them believe he had not taken the canoe and motor. The instant he set foot on shore at home, he would be caught red-handed, whether they happened to see him come up or not.

As he drew closer to the border, his apprehension increased—but for a different reason. He was actually entering the country illegally, just as he had gone into the States illegally several hours before. The OPP didn't get over to that part of the Angle often, but they did show up occasionally—and without warning.

Slipping across the border was simple and only took a moment. On other occasions, it had not bothered him at all, but this time sweat stood out on his forehead, and his heart raced. Danny Orlis wouldn't do a thing like that, no matter what. Steve felt as though everyone within a hundred miles knew what he was doing and was watching him.

In the distance, he could see a boat heading his direction. At first it was just a speck on the horizon—so small he wasn't sure whether he was imagining it or not. As the minutes passed, however, it continued to grow until there was no mistaking it. The speeding craft skimmed between the islands and swept toward him.

"This is it!" he told himself miserably. The officers must have been watching with field glasses from some concealed vantage point. They must have seen him come over from the American side. He was caught this time and was in genuine trouble—the sort of trouble even his mum couldn't get him out of.

His first thought was to turn and race back to where he came from as fast as he could, but he realized that was useless. There was no way he could get back across the border in time to elude the boat that was fast approaching. If only he had taken time to go by Customs and enter the States and leave legally. If only he hadn't disobeyed his grandfather, he wouldn't be in this trouble! If–If–If–

But he had disobeyed. He had broken the law. And this time he would not be able to lie out of it! His heart hammered fiercely against his ribs, and his breath came in sharp, quick stabs. Steve had never been so frightened in all his life.

* * * *

Back home, Danny Orlis filleted the fish his party caught, packed them in plastic bags, and placed them in the freezer. Then he and Grant took the waste to the big, shallow pit that had been dug for that purpose and covered it with dirt.

"There," Danny said, straightening. "That job's done for another day."

"Going to be guiding tomorrow?" Grant asked.

Danny shook his head. "I don't know for sure, but I don't think so. Those guys are good fishermen. All they needed was to know where to go."

A smile burst across Grant's features. "Man! Have I got news for you! You and I are going fishing with Steve Driscoll tomorrow."

Danny's eyes narrowed curiously. "Is that why he came over this afternoon?"

"That's why. He said he found a place where the fish are biting like you've never seen before. Big stuff!"

Danny's expression did not change.

"What's the matter?" his cousin demanded.

"Aren't you excited?"

"Excited?" he echoed. "That depends."

"You don't get it, Danny!" Grant said. "He's going to show us where they are! He's taking us right to the spot!"

Danny still did not respond as his cousin thought he should. The smile left Grant's lips. "Is there something I don't know about?" he asked. "Something that's going to keep us from going fishing with Steve tomorrow?"

"Not as far as I know. I was just thinking about Steve. Maybe he's found a good place to fish—and maybe he hasn't."

"But he said he'd never seen anything like it."

"I know he said those things, but he doesn't always tell the truth. He could have been stringing you along so he could get us over there."

Grant turned that over in his mind. "Do you *really* think he'd do that?" he asked.

"Don't you?"

Grant had to admit that he did if lying about the fishing would suit his purpose.

"But we'll sure go over and see if he's telling the truth," Danny continued.

Grant grinned. "This is one time I sure hope he is."

* * * *

Steve kept eyeing the boat that raced toward him, scarcely daring to breathe. It was still three-quarters of a mile away, but he began to wonder if it was a government boat after all. It was moving faster than any he had observed, for one thing, and it had a different profile. At the moment, he couldn't quite place what was different about it, but there was something that wasn't quite the same. As it sped closer, he could see why. It rode lower in the water, for one thing. It was considerably smaller, and it slammed across the lake like a bullet.

At that instant, the driver of the boat waved, and Steve expelled his breath with a rush. It wasn't the OPP after all. It was only Peter Starr!

He stopped the canoe with a twist of the throttle and waved in return. The jet slammed close and squatted in the water as Peter cut the speed.

"Hi."

Steve grinned his relief. "Am I glad it's you! I thought for a minute the OPP had me."

His friend grinned. "What've you been doing now?"

"I went over to the American side and didn't bother to clear Customs. When I saw you coming, I was sure they had me."

Peter laughed. "Don't worry. It's like I told you, you're stupid to travel all the way over there just to go into American water. They'll never catch you. I go back and forth all the time. Only had to hide once."

"I guess maybe you're right," he said doubtfully.

"I *know* I'm right. You stick to me, Steve! I'll teach you the ropes!"

The younger boy turned his attention to the boat. "A new one, eh?"

"Yeah," Peter laughed cynically. "Had a little trouble with the steering on the old crate the other day. I told Dad I was afraid to drive it anymore. Was scared I'd pile her up on the rocks. So we went in to Kenora and bought this baby." He patted the gleaming hull. "And will she ever go! There's nothing faster on the whole lake! Not even at Kenora or Warroad."

"There was nothing any faster than your other one," Steve told him.

"I know." He dismissed it with a wave of his hand. "But this little number would go by the old one like she was standing still!"

Steve eyed it wistfully. "I sure wish I had a boat like that."

Peter winked at him. "You've got to be lucky—like me!"

He paused and leaned forward. "We're going to have to get together again one of these days."

Steve nodded. "Sounds good." He didn't know what his grandfather would say to that. He disliked Peter Starr more than any of his grandson's other friends. He didn't like Peter, and he especially didn't like his boat. Claimed the roar scared all the fish within half a mile. But Steve wouldn't let the old man stop him. He'd see Peter any time he wanted to!

The older boy acted as though he had something else on his mind, but he didn't mention it until he was ready to leave.

"I've been looking for that Orlis character," he said, his fingers on the ignition key. "Seen 'im around today?"

"He was going home as I left their place," Steve said. "He guided some fishermen today."

Peter swore under his breath. "I *knew* I should've gone over on that side!" He lowered his voice. "You gonna see him again soon?"

Steve was about to tell his friend about the fishing the next day, but he read the disapproval in Peter's eyes.

"Maybe," he said carelessly.

"If I don't get to see him first, will you tell him something for me?"

"Sure." For an instant, jealousy gripped the younger boy to think that Peter might be Danny's friend, too. He had had the idea that he was the only friend Peter had on the lake. To learn that he was wrong upset him.

"Tell him to keep his mouth shut!"

Steve's eyes widened. *"What did you say?"*

"Tell him to keep his mouth shut if he knows what's good for him!"

Then, before the boy in the canoe could say more, Peter started the engine, shoved the throttle forward, and blasted away—causing the frail canoe to rock violently.

When Steve got back home, his grandfather was in the house. Just as he suspected, the old man heard him approach. He came to the door and watched as the boy pulled the craft up on shore, removed the motor, and turned the canoe over. Grimly, he squared his shoulders and carried the light motor to the shed where it was kept.

Just let the old man try to jump down his throat for going over to see Danny and Grant. Let him try it! He had taken all he was going to from his mum and his grandfather. If they kept getting on his back about everything he did, he'd run away! He'd show them! He'd show them both! He'd get out of there, and they'd have to find someone else to bully!

The only reason they kept him there was so they could order him around. *Steve! Run down to the lake for a pail of water. Steve! Go out to the garden and weed the potatoes. Steve! Help me lift the nets!*

If it wasn't for all the work they got out of him, they wouldn't even keep him around. They sure didn't do it because they thought anything of him. He was a slave, that's what he was! An unpaid slave!

He was sure his grandfather was going to jump him as soon as he got to the house—and he was ready for it—but he didn't. Tom LeFevre sat in a chair near the window, staring morosely out at the lake. It was obvious to Steve that he wasn't going to say anything, either. He had something else on his mind.

"I'm glad you got home, Stephen," his mum said when he entered the sparsely furnished house. "Go in and wash. Supper's ready."

At the table, his grandfather said little. Even Steve's mum noticed it.

"Dad," she said, "are you alright?"

He looked up suddenly. "Me? Sure. I'm fine. Why wouldn't I be?"

"You've hardly eaten a thing."

"I'm not hungry," he growled.

"You didn't eat much at noon, either."

"What is this, the third degree?" He pushed his chair back from the table. "Can't a man have a little peace in his own house without somebody nagging at him all the time?" he demanded.

Her temper flared. "I just wanted to know if you were sick!"

"Well, I'm not! Now shut up, will you?"

They finished the meal in silence.

It was not until they were leaving the table that LeFevre turned to his grandson. "When I call you in the morning, get yourself out of bed—and be quick about it!"

"How come?" the boy asked defiantly.

"Because I say so! That's why! We're going out to lift my nets, and you're going to help! Understand?"

Steve's lips trembled, and he looked plaintively at his mum, expecting her to intervene—but she said nothing.

"It isn't going to do you any good to look at your mum! She's not going to talk me out of it this time! You're going to start working around here!"

The boy nodded, but his resentment grew. They were going to push him too far some time! Then they'd be sorry!

CHAPTER 7

THE LONELY BOY

The next morning when Tom LeFevre got up, the wind was whipping across the bay, lacing the swells with foam. Clouds had moved in sometime during the night and hid the blue of the sky. The dark gray covering added a certain oppressive chill to the air and a threat of rain, as a few scattered drops splattered on the roof and the thirsty garden behind the house. For a time, he sat on the side of the bed, staring across the little room.

If someone had put a hex on him, it would begin to show up that morning. The spirits didn't fool around. They either set to work as soon as they had been summoned or they remained asleep. There was nothing halfway about their reactions. He got to his feet and dressed thoughtfully, putting on a flannel shirt over his long underwear. He was almost afraid to go out on the lake and start lifting his nets that morning.

If the hex was very powerful—and he had to accept the fact that it could be—he might smash a hole in the bottom of his boat on a reef or lose his footing and fall overboard. Hitting rocks would be bad enough, but falling in would be disastrous. He couldn't swim a stroke.

He stood in the doorway a few minutes. He should go out, lift his nets, and quit fishing until that business with the hex was settled. But he couldn't. He had Rachel and her kid to look after, and with little enough cash. If he couldn't catch fish, there would be no gas and oil for his motor—and little food.

There was the garden, of course, and the fish Rachel had smoked when his catches were good. For one person, the stores would last for a month or more. For three, it would melt away in days. What then?

He went to the living room and stared down at his grandson asleep on the sofa bed. He didn't want to take Stephen along on the lake that morning. The boy was just like that worthless dad of his. Looked like him and acted like him. He even worked like him, which meant that he did as little as possible. They were both good for nothing.

But if he didn't make Stephen go along, he would have to be out there alone, facing whatever trouble the spirits cooked up for him. He shook his head in resignation. The boy wouldn't be much help, but at least he would be company. And there was just a chance that the spirits would not be so vicious with his grandson there.

"Stephen!" he said, stooping down to shake him by the shoulder. "It's time to get up."

The boy groaned and closed his eyes even tighter.

"Stephen!" LeFevre said, his voice getting louder. "It's time to go out and lift the nets! Get up this minute, or I'll wallop you!"

Grumbling, the boy shook the sleep from his head and sat up, reaching for his jeans.

"Move it!" his grandfather ordered. "It looks like rain!"

He got as far as the door before looking back. The instant he turned away, Stephen had lain down once more and was asleep. Tom LeFevre swore and stormed back to the sofa bed, reaching angrily for his grandson's leg and jerking him to the floor.

"Now get dressed and get down to the boat before I club you!"

"All right! All right!" The boy put on his shirt and pants. "I don't know why you have to pick on *me* all the time! I ain't done nothin' to you!"

"You ain't done nothin' *for* me, either! Now shut up and get into them boots, or we'll be out on the lake in the rain."

Stephen was hungry and wanted to eat breakfast before they left, but he knew better than to say anything about that. He had already pushed his grandfather as far as he dared.

By the time they reached the boat, the rain had stopped, the wind was beginning to die, and holes were being torn in the clouds as they skittered over the forest in the direction of Kenora. Streaks of blue sky were showing.

Lifting the nets was wet, cold work, and they had to be dressed for it. The old man stepped into the fishing scow, pulled two rubber rain suits from the locker, and tossed one to his grandson.

"We'll be needing these," he said. "We'd just as well put them on now."

The boy did as he was told and joined his grandfather in the boat. They pushed away from the dock and poled the clumsy craft out into deeper water before LeFevre lowered the big outboard and started it with the ignition key.

Remembering that Danny and Grant were meeting him on the island at ten, Stephen glanced apprehensively at his watch. It was later than he thought. He wanted to ask if they would be back in time—but he didn't dare.

"How long is this going to take, anyway?" he asked instead.

His grandfather grunted his disapproval. "What do you care? You aren't going anywhere."

The boy's temper flared. "I don't like to spend *all* my time out here lifting nets."

"You like to eat, don't you?" LeFevre muttered.

Maybe it wouldn't take all that long today, the elderly Indian told himself. Maybe the hex was working and he wouldn't catch much. Grimly, he forced the thought from his mind, directing his attention to the task at hand.

The nets were set quite close to the dock, and in ten minutes they had reached the first one. The old man's pulse quickened as he throttled down the motor and shifted to neutral. They glided to the flag that marked one end of the long gill net. Stephen stood in the bow, grasped the flag with both hands, and lifted the buoy that carried it. Hurriedly he pushed the prow of the fishing boat beneath the net lines, and they set to work pulling the nylon mesh across the boat and removing the fish.

LeFevre had put on his heavy rubber gloves and was using the short-handled hook to pull the net strands from the bellies of the plump, round suckers and walleyes. The former couldn't be sold and were thrown into the water to be eaten by the gulls and pelicans. The latter were tossed into one of the plastic boxes they had brought along for that purpose.

It seemed to Stephen that there were as many fish as ever, but his grandfather was not satisfied. From time to time, he stopped long enough to ice the walleyes in the box. But the frown on his wrinkled face deepened as they moved from one net to another.

"I knew it!" he exclaimed when they finished. "I knew we wouldn't have a good catch today."

Stephen glanced up at him. "I thought we did all right."

LeFevre shook his head. "*They* wouldn't shut the fishing off all at once." He spoke more to himself than to his youthful companion. "They'd cut it down just enough to let me know what was happening—allowing me to catch a few so I would think I could work through it. Then—bam!" He slammed his fist into his open hand. "No more fish! No more game! No *nothing* for me!"

Stephen's eyes widened curiously. "Who's going to do all that to us?"

The old man shook his head. "Never mind. You wouldn't understand."

His grandson bristled. "How do you *know* I wouldn't? Just try me!"

LeFevre jerked up. "Shut that big mouth of yours before I whop you!"

Sullenly Stephen settled back in the seat, fuming inwardly. He didn't know what was the matter with that granddad of his. Treated him like he was two years old and didn't know anything.

Rachel Driscoll was up and had breakfast ready by the time they got back and had the fish properly packed and iced and ready to ship. Stephen ate hurriedly, wondering as he did so how he was going to manage to slip away to meet Danny and his cousin. With his granddad on the warpath, he was sure to be in trouble, whatever he did.

But the elderly Indian was so preoccupied, he acted as though his grandson wasn't even there. As soon as they finished breakfast, he got to his feet and stormed outside. The boy went to the window and watched him pause on the edge of the clearing, then look around before walking into the woods and disappearing from view.

"What's wrong with him now?" Rachel demanded of her son. "Did you two have another fight when you were out on the lake this morning? Did you lip off to him again?"

"No, I didn't lip off to him again," Stephen retorted defensively. "I don't see why you have to blame *me* for everything! I can't do anything right!" His lips trembled as though he was about to start crying. "You're as bad as he is!"

His mom's features darkened. "Stephen, I'm warning you! One more crack, and you'll spend the rest of the day in the house helping me!"

His eyes narrowed as he tried to gauge whether she meant what she had said. He didn't think she did. She was always saying things like that. But today he couldn't risk it. If he did, he would get stuck in the house and miss out on a good fishing trip.

* * * *

Danny Orlis and his cousin got up early that morning, put the motors back on the boats that would be used that day, and saw that they were filled with gas. As soon as breakfast was over, they got their fishing gear, climbed into the *Scappoose*, and shoved off.

"Think we can make it to the island to meet Steve by ten o'clock?" Grant asked, glancing uneasily at his watch.

"Sure. It's only nine now."

Leaving the mouth of Pine Creek, they angled diagonally across the bay toward the Customs Houses. The officer on duty on the Canadian side stopped them this time and questioned them briefly.

From there, the boys went straight to the island where they were to meet their friend. "We're a little late," Grant said. "Think he'll still be there?"

For answer, Danny pointed at the canoe pulled up on shore in a little cove to their right. "He's there all right."

As they drew closer and could see his face plainly, his features brightened and he waved to them.

The *Scappoose* grated on the rocky bottom several feet from shore, and Stephen snatched up his old fishing rod and battered tackle box. With them in hand, he waded into the water with his runners on.

"I see you didn't forget your tackle," Danny said, grinning.

"No way! You can't catch fish without tackle." He clambered into the boat, the legs of his jeans wet half to his knees. "I was scared you guys weren't coming."

"Weren't coming?" Grant echoed. "I said we'd be here, didn't I?"

"We wouldn't miss a chance to catch all those fish you were telling Grant about."

Stephen Driscoll straightened. "You think I was feeding you a line about those fish, don't you?"

"We'll soon know," Danny told him. "Just guide us over there and get out of our way!"

"I'll show you there are fish around this island! Take us over to those rushes and start casting."

They did as he directed.

Grant was the first to get a lure into the water. As soon as it splatted noisily on the rippled surface, there was a swirl as a gigantic northern pike rushed for it. Grant's rod arced, and line spun from his reel.

"I've got 'im! I've got 'im!" he chortled, shoving the butt of the long, spin-casting rod into the pit of his stomach. The fish was far from exhausted, and Grant had a difficult time wearing him down enough for Danny to get the net under him. But at last the big pike lay motionless in the water, and Danny lifted him into the boat with the net.

"Look at him!" Grant cried, removing the fish from the hook and holding him up for his companions to admire. "He weighs ten pounds if he weighs an ounce."

"You're right about that," Danny said. "He's a nice fish. A real nice fish!"

"What'd I tell you?" Stephen chortled. "I found this place myself, and I haven't told anybody else about it."

That was only the beginning. Danny caught three northerns, and Grant and Stephen each got another before they moved to the far end of the island to fish for walleyes off the rocks. The fishing was excellent there as well, and by midafternoon the boys were close to their limit. Danny decided they should return home.

"The fish are still biting great," Stephen said. "We don't want to quit now."

"We'll be over our limit if we do," Danny told him.

Young Driscoll stared at him. "Who's to know? I've been living here the last two months and haven't even *seen* a game warden. They're not going to start coming around now. You can take all the fish you want. No one will ever find out."

"We will," Danny said simply. "And so will God."

"Now what kind of a stupid remark is that?"

"It isn't a stupid remark. It's the truth. Even if no one else ever finds out that we've broken the law by taking too many fish, we will know it—and so will God. That's reason enough not to do it."

Stephen frowned. "I've never met anyone like you. You've got to have rocks in your head." He reeled in his line and removed the lure. "But if you insist on quitting, it's okay with me."

"I agree with you, Steve," Grant said. "We might never have another chance like this."

"We know where to come now," Danny told him. "We can come back any time."

Grant was about to cast once more, but his cousin warned him not to. "Pack it in," he said firmly. "We're quitting."

Grant didn't like it, but Danny had already started the motor and was waiting for him to sit down before leaving for Stephen's canoe. He was still muttering under his breath when Danny shut off the engine and glided toward the light craft.

"We could just as well have caught a few more fish," Stephen said as he got out to wade ashore.

"Would you like to learn more about why I feel as I do about breaking the law?" Danny asked.

"Not particularly."

Danny ignored the remark. "We have Sunday school and church at the schoolhouse every Sunday afternoon. We'd sure like to have you come."

Stephen looked back to face them. "Will you guys be there?"

Grant started to say he didn't know, but Danny spoke quickly. "We'll be there."

"I might come, at that."

"It starts at three o'clock."

CHAPTER 8

THE OLD WAYS

Danny and his cousin waited until Stephen pushed the canoe back into the water and got in. Then they started the engine, and the *Scappoose* roared up the bay in the direction of the American Customs House where they would have to stop.

"That was some fishing trip," Grant said, looking down at the big northern pike he had caught on his first cast.

"It was neat, wasn't it? We'll have to go back and try it again in a couple of days."

"We can't go too soon to suit me."

They stopped briefly at Customs, then made their way to Pine Creek and the Orlis place.

"I sure hope Steve comes over to Sunday school and church this week," Danny said.

Grant eyed him curiously. "Why should you care?" he asked.

"He needs Jesus as his Savior," young Orlis replied. "He needs to confess his sin and put his trust in Christ."

"How do you know he's a sinner?" the other boy persisted. "He didn't seem so bad to me, except for the way he fought with his granddad. We might do the same thing if we got treated the way he did."

"The Bible tells us that we all have sinned and come short of the glory of God," Danny said. "We're sinners, regardless of how good we try to be. We have to confess our sin and put our trust in Christ if we want to go to Heaven when we die."

For an instant or two, Grant acted as though he was about to voice other questions that bothered him, but he didn't. The look in his eyes indicated that he still didn't understand what Danny was saying. Still, he changed the subject, talking about the work they had to do when they got home. The opportunity for Danny to continue to share Christ with him was gone.

Back at the LeFevre cabin, no one seemed to notice when Stephen came home. His grandfather was sitting on a rickety bench, leaning against the icehouse and staring at the distant clouds. A frown deepened the lines in his seamed face. The boy, certain that he was in for a beating, slunk past the old man. But LeFevre acted as though he scarcely saw him. His gnarled hands were busy braiding a grass that was common to the area.

His grandson was so curious he stopped beside him, his eyes widening.

"What're you doing?" he asked.

LeFevre turned, his aged, wrinkled features suddenly alive.

"You really want to know?"

Stephen was so surprised at the tone of his grandfather's voice that he stepped backward involuntarily.

"It's no big deal."

He would have gone on up to the house, but his grandfather stopped him. "Sit down."

"I ain't got time."

"I said, 'Sit down!' I've got to talk to you!"

Uneasily, the boy did as he was told. He had never seen his grandfather in such a mood before. He was usually angry and difficult to be around. Now he acted as though he wanted to talk.

"I should talk to you," the old man continued earnestly. "I should have talked to you a long time ago." He looked away again toward the distant shore. "Maybe that's the reason for the hex. The spirits could be angry with me because I haven't taught anyone to carry on with worshiping them and bringing them gifts when I am gone. Now I'm in trouble and am apt to be robbed!"

Stephen squirmed and wished he could get away. He remembered his mum telling how her dad had summoned the spirits and talked with them when she was a little girl. He had listened, feeling the cold chills dance up and down his back, but he always thought that was something that had happened a long time ago. Way back before he was born.

"When I was a boy," LeFevre continued, "the old witch doctor used to say it was very important that the young ones were taught the ways of the spirits. But I quit doing much of that business when I got old. I didn't have any sons, and that disagreeable mum of yours wouldn't do anything I wanted her to. He paused significantly. "Now the spirits are angry. Maybe that is the reason."

Stephen moistened his lips with the tip of his tongue and twisted to look to either side, as though expecting the spirits to appear at any moment. He didn't believe all that stuff. At least he didn't *think* he believed it.

"I–I've got to go!" he said quickly, getting to his feet. "I think Mum wants me!"

The old man stretched out twisted fingers to clutch his wrist, but the boy eluded his grasp and retreated just beyond his grandfather's reach.

LeFevre ignored his protest.

"Know what I'm doing?" he asked in a tone as friendly as he had ever used in addressing his grandson. "I'm braiding sweet grass to use with tobacco. I use it to call my spirit."

Steve backed away, fear glinting in his eyes. "I–I–"

"I will teach you how to summon the spirits," LeFevre said. "Then you can choose one among the spirits that come to you in your spirit dream. She will help you all your life. All you have to do is remember to worship her and give her gifts."

The boy continued to retreat.

"Don't leave yet, Stephen! There is much to learn!"

That was as much as the boy could take. He whirled and dashed up to the house where his mom was preparing supper.

"Did you see your grandfather?"

He nodded. "What's with the old man, anyway?" His voice was still trembling. "He's weird!"

"What do you mean?"

"He was talking to me about the spirits and getting them to come to him by burning tobacco and sweet grass." Stephen shivered. "It gave me the creeps."

She smiled. "I felt the same way when I was your age and he used to hang cloth and jewelry and hunting knives out in the bush for his spirit, the loon."

Stephen paused. "He wanted me to do that crazy stuff. Said he'd teach me!"

With that, he went over to the table, pulled out a rickety chair, and sat down. He was still shaken by the encounter with his grandfather.

"Weird!" he repeated under his breath.

She put another piece of wood in the stove and filled the coffeepot with water from the bucket nearby. "He used to want me to do that, too, but I ran and hid when I thought he was going to try to teach me."

Stephen sat for a long while, staring down at the table. "Is it for real?" he demanded. "Does he really and truly talk to the spirits?"

His mom worked in silence for several minutes before turning back to her son. "I've asked myself the same thing a thousand times," she said thoughtfully. "I know *he* believes it's real. And I have to admit he's been able to do some strange things that he said worked out because his spirit helped him." She got the dishes and set the table. "But I was always so afraid when he started talking to me about doing it that I wouldn't listen. Like I said, I'd run and hide."

The corners of Stephen's mouth tightened. "He's not going to get me trying that stuff, either!" he exclaimed. "I'll run and hide the way you used to!"

She nodded approvingly.

It was good to have her on his side in a disagreement with his grandfather, he decided. Most of the time, she was on his back something fierce every time he said anything.

LeFevre came into the house a few minutes before supper was ready. He went to a small room that opened off the kitchen, unlocked the padlock that held the door secure against anyone save himself, and went inside—carrying the braided sweet grass in his hand. He returned a moment later, relocked the door, and sat down.

Stephen could feel the old man's sharp gaze boring into him, but he did not look up. He was sure his grandfather was going to talk to him about the spirits and getting one of his own, but he didn't. Instead, he stood suddenly and approached his daughter.

"Know where that cloth is?" he asked. "The one I bought the last time we had Orlis pick up some things for us in Warroad?"

She shook her head. "You took charge of it as soon as we got it. Said this was one piece I wasn't going to get to make a dress of."

That seemed to satisfy him. "I remember now. It's in there with the rest of my things!" He turned back to the locked door and fumbled with the key for a moment before freeing the lock so he could go inside. He was back almost immediately. "It's there all right."

Rachel motioned for him to come to the table.

"I've about got my things together," he said. "Stephen and I are going to be busy the next few days."

The boy's face went ashen, and his lips trembled. "No way," he muttered.

Tom LeFevre glared at the boy. "You'll do as I say! I know now why the spirits are angry! They want me to teach you to worship them! And that's what I'm fixing to do!"

"You won't neither!" Rachel broke in fiercely. "I won't stand for it!"

LeFevre shrank away involuntarily, as though she had slapped him.

"He don't want to do it!" she repeated. "And he don't have to! He's *my* kid! I'll tell him what to do!"

The old man shook his head incredulously. "You know what the spirits are doing to me, don't you? You know how few fish we got today!" He drew a deep breath. "And you know I ain't been able to sneak up on any game for two weeks! There's a hex on me! And that's the way to get the spirits to bring my luck back! They'll be so pleased about Stephen that we'll have plenty to eat and plenty of cash in our pockets! The hex will be gone, and everything will be fine for us again!"

She snorted her derision.

Instead of answering, he pushed back the chair noisily, got to his feet, and stormed outside.

"What do we do now?" Stephen asked, still trembling at the thought of what his grandfather wanted to start teaching him. He didn't know why it upset him so much, but it did.

His mom glanced at the door, then back at her son. "We'll sit down and eat, of course," she said, answering his question. "He'll come back when he's hungry!"

Before the meal was finished, old LeFevre stomped in. He looked at neither of them as he pulled out his chair and sat down. Anger and fear mingled in his eyes, and the corners of his mouth turned down.

"If something bad happens on account of this, Rachel," he snapped, "it's your fault. It'll be all your fault!"

* * * *

Danny and Grant wanted to go back to the fishing spot Stephen showed them, but they weren't able to find time that week. New guests came in, requiring Danny's services as a guide for two days. Another party had motor trouble, and Carl Orlis had to spend Saturday working on the engine. That left Danny with the responsibility of guiding again. When he got back home the last afternoon following a long day of guiding, Grant came down to help him clean fish.

"Sure wish we'd hooked this bunch," his cousin said. "Where'd you get 'em? Over at Steve's?"

Danny shook his head. "That's on the Canadian side, and my fishermen weren't licensed over there."

"Think we can make it before long?"

Danny nodded. "If Steve comes over for church tomorrow, we'll try to work things out so he can go with us. We don't need him, but he showed us the spot. The least we can do is take him along."

The next afternoon when Danny and his cousin reached the schoolhouse where services were to be held, Steve was already there. He came down to the dock to meet them.

"Hey, you made it!" Danny exclaimed. "That's cool."

"I had to sneak away," he retorted. "That ornery granddad of mine was sure mad this morning." He shook his head. "It was bad!"

About that time, Carl and Mary Orlis arrived, and everyone went inside for the service. Danny didn't know what Stephen thought, but he did listen attentively. One of the group led the singing, and another spoke. When church was over, they divided into Sunday school classes for another hour. Toward the end, Stephen began to fidget uneasily.

"How much longer is this going on, Danny?" he whispered, leaning over to his friend.

"It'll be over in a few minutes."

He settled back in the chair but continued to fidget. As soon as the class was over, he got to his feet and started for the door.

"How about going fishing with us tomorrow?" Grant asked.

Stephen paused. "I'd like to. Only–"

"Only what?"

"I don't know what he'll say about it!" He looked at his watch. "I've got to go! I may be in big trouble already."

"We'll meet at the same place and the same time tomorrow morning," Danny said. "If you're late, go over where we'll be fishing. If we're late, we'll do the same."

Stephen Driscoll nodded and headed for the boat he had used. There were times, like this one, when nothing he did satisfied his grandfather. On those occasions, he wouldn't get yelled at anymore for using the fishing boat than for taking the canoe—if the old man was of a mind to jump on him, that is. If he wasn't, he wouldn't say anything—regardless of what he had done.

It seemed to take longer than ever that afternoon to get back to the place where he and his mom were living. He went around by Customs, for one thing, and that was several miles farther. For another, he bucked a head wind part of the way and waves that wouldn't quit. Finally he reached the protection of the islands. It went better after that.

As far as he could remember, that was the first time he had ever been to church. He had heard people use the name of God and Jesus Christ in swearing but never the way those people used them. When they talked about either one, they talked as though they loved Him. He didn't understand much of what that speaker said, but whatever it was, he felt that he wanted to learn more about Jesus and God. It really made a guy curious.

CHAPTER 9

STAY AWAY FROM ORLIS

When Steve got home again, his grandfather was sitting on the bench behind the icehouse, waiting for him with growing impatience. The old man's scowl was dark and ominous, shouting trouble for his grandson. He did not move as Stephen tied the boat to the dock, taking longer than necessary. When the boy looked up, he was still glaring.

"Who said you could take that boat?" he growled—so harshly that the dog at his feet slunk away.

Stephen did not reply. He was in for it this time, but he half suspected he would be. For the last day or so, his grandfather had been surly and ill-tempered.

"And where've you been?"

Stephen's lips curled bitterly. "On the lake."

"Where on the lake?"

"Just around."

"And what's that supposed to mean?" he demanded.

Stephen planted both feet squarely on the dock, defiance in every move.

"You're not my boss! I don't have to tell you anything!"

"I may not be your boss, young man, but that boat belongs to me! You've got to get *my* permission before you use it! Is that clear?"

Stephen recoiled slightly, but there was no change in the tone of his voice.

"Go ahead! Beat me for it! That's what you're working up to, ain't it?"

His grandfather took a step toward him. "I don't need *you* to tell me what to do! You take that boat again without my knowin' it and you'll get a walloping you won't forget!"

Sensing that nothing serious was going to happen, the boy took a step forward. "Mum won't let you!" he taunted.

"She ain't got nothin' to say about it," LeFevre retorted defensively. "As long as you're puttin' your feet under my table, you'll do as I tell you!"

The boy moved forward cautiously, uneasy about having to pass so close to the old man. He didn't think he was going to be hit, but he couldn't be sure. It was close. Too close to suit him. One wrong remark, one wrong inflection in his voice, even one wrong move could cause his grandfather to explode.

His heart was hammering, and his body was taut as a tightly wound spring. Four more steps, three, two, would be enough to take him out of his grandfather's reach. He was congratulating himself on his success when it happened. A gnarled hand snaked out and jerked a printed Sunday school paper from his pocket.

"What's this?" LeFevre snapped.

Heart sinking, Stephen lunged for it desperately. But with surprising swiftness old LeFevre moved his hand behind him.

"That's mine!" the boy snarled. "You've got no right to take it!"

"Where'd you get it?"

He hesitated. He wanted to lie—to tell his grandfather that he had found the Sunday school paper, or that somebody pressed him so hard that he shoved it into his pocket without even looking at it. Yet he knew that would never work. His grandfather was old and had spent little time in school—but he wasn't easy to fool. He always said he could *smell* a lie, and there were times when Stephen half believed him.

"Carl Orlis gave it to me," he admitted reluctantly.

"So!" He moved backward half a step and eyed the paper, reading the title page aloud. "A *Sunday School Take-home Paper*. That's where you were! Over at that church service they hold every Sunday afternoon!"

Stephen remained silent.

"I might've known it when that Orlis brat came over here!"

"He didn't have nothin' to do with it!" Stephen retorted lamely.

LeFevre's gaze was fixed on his grandson. "Don't try to tell me that! I've been around them Orlises myself! I *know* what they're like!"

Stephen's lips quivered, and he shrank from his grandfather. "You don't have to believe me if you don't want to," he pouted.

"For once you just told the truth! I don't have to believe you if I don't want to. I *know* when I'm being lied to!" He swore angrily. "Now get up to the house before I whop you good!"

Reluctantly the boy did as he was told.

"And don't leave until I tell you!" LeFevre shouted after him. "I ain't done with you yet!"

Stephen knew that this was not the time to do anything else that might increase the old man's wrath. He made his way up the path to the house. By the time he went inside, his grandfather was two steps behind him.

"Know where that kid of yours was today?" LeFevre demanded of his daughter.

She sighed, shrugging helplessly.

"He went over to that *church* that Orlis family goes to." His lips curled bitterly.

Rachel went to the stove and stirred the fire. She didn't know why her dad hounded her about Stephen all the time. He ought to realize by now that she couldn't handle her son. He did as he pleased.

"Ain't you going to do anything about it?"

"What do you expect me to do about that?" she asked defensively. "There ain't no law against going to church."

The old man shook his head. "I might have known I'd get an answer like that from you. Always sticking up for him! I've got enough trouble on my hands without him making things worse by going to church!"

"Like what?"

"The spirits are so mad now they let somebody put a hex on me, and they'll let that crook steal me blind if things like this keep on happening." He sagged into a chair beside the table and ordered his daughter to fix him a cup of tea. "I ought to beat him good," he muttered, glaring at his grandson.

"I only went because Danny asked me," Stephen retorted. "It sure wasn't my idea."

"That's no excuse!"

"A boy's got to have *some* friends," Rachel broke in. "You said that yourself."

"It don't have to be that Danny Orlis. He can get *other* friends. Plenty of them."

"Where?" his daughter demanded. She poured a steeping cup of tea and set it before her dad. "I haven't seen any other boys close by," she persisted, "except that Peter—whatever his name is. And you said yourself that you didn't want Stephen running with him."

LeFevre grunted his indignation. "At least *he* wouldn't get the spirits so riled up they'd turn on me.

Stephen glanced at his mom narrowly, trying to decide whether she was going to continue to defend him. When she said no more, he decided it was time for him to speak. Almost past time. Somebody had to do something to quiet his grandfather. He had never seen the old man so angry.

"I'm not going over to that church again," he said. "It was boring."

It really hadn't been. He was lying once more. Some of the things that were said about Jesus and sin tore at his heart. But he couldn't let his grandfather know that. It would be the surest way he could think of to get a beating.

It was as though the old man hadn't even heard what he said. He remained motionless, staring numbly into space. At last he stood and limped over to Stephen. "If I catch you with Danny Orlis once more," he grated, "you're not going to stay with me. Not one more day! Not even an hour!" He directed his attention to his daughter. "That goes for you, too."

She glared at him but remained quiet.

The following morning, LeFevre got Stephen out of bed to help lift the nets. It was earlier than he usually went out, and there was a chill in the air. A thin, filmy mist dulled the brightness of the sun and hid the tree-lined shores of the nearest islands. The lonely call of a loon drifted to them, marring the breathless hush of early morning.

"Hear that?" the old man asked, a smile lifting the corners of his mouth. "That's an omen! A sign that my spirit is pleased with me." He paused. For the first time in days, he sounded pleasant and agreeable. "And with you, too, Stephen," he added. "My spirit, the loon, was mad at you because you refused to follow the old ways and become a witch doctor. Then you went to church yesterday, which made her furious." He smiled expansively. "But now that you aren't going back, she is appeased. We'll soon know if she is pleased enough to let me get my luck back." He drew in a deep breath. "Maybe she'll even protect us from being robbed. Wouldn't that be great?"

They did a little better fishing that morning, and the old man brightened. "What did I tell you, Stephen? She is pleased with us." He removed a plump walleye from the net and tossed it into the fish box. "Not well enough to give us a good catch, mind you. She wants us to know that she has been angry but is beginning to get over it."

It was then that the boy remembered he had made arrangements to go fishing with Danny and Grant. He glanced up at the sun. There was plenty of time to get away from the house and meet them if that grandfather of his didn't keep him out on the lake too long. He had promised the old man that he would stay away from Danny Orlis, but he had no intention of doing so. What his grandfather didn't know wouldn't hurt him. It didn't matter that seeing his friend would make him a liar again. All he cared about was being clever enough to avoid being caught.

* * * *

At the Orlis home, Danny and Grant had finished breakfast and were hurrying to get their work done in time to meet Stephen and go fishing that morning.

"Think old LeFevre'll let him go with us?" Grant asked as Danny got out the power mower and filled it with gas.

Young Orlis straightened slowly. "I'm afraid he's planning to sneak away again."

"So?"

"I got to thinking about it last night after devotions. We're not doing what we should when we help him deceive his grandfather."

Grant's eyes narrowed. "I don't see that that's any concern of ours. It isn't our fault the old man is so cantankerous."

"When we met Steve on the island the other day," Danny continued, "we were helping him to lie about where he was and what he was doing. We're as guilty as he is."

His cousin did not agree with Danny. "I don't get it," he said, his eyes narrowing.

Danny started the mower and set to work. He was still troubled by what he and his cousin had done— what they were going to do again that morning by meeting the young Indian boy on an island so his cranky old grandfather wouldn't know about it.

Grant was right when he said LeFevre shouldn't be so hard on Steve. A guy ought to be able to go fishing with his friends once in a while without having to lie about what he was doing. Yet that didn't give them the right to help the boy deceive the old man.

When he got right down to it, Danny realized that it was really his responsibility. He was the Christian. He ought to be an example to the others. He had already confessed what he had done and had asked God's forgiveness. Now he had to see Steve about it. His new friend probably wouldn't understand any more than Grant had, but that didn't matter.

Young Orlis was still trying to decide how to go about it when he finished mowing and he and Grant helped clean cabins. Then they were ready to go out on the lake.

"Suppose Steve's already over at the island waiting for us?" Grant asked as they got into the boat and pushed away from the dock.

"I hope so."

There was a strange tone in Danny's voice—a tone that disturbed his cousin.

"What do you mean by that?"

"I've got to talk to him."

"About what?" Grant demanded suspiciously.

"I've got to tell him I'm sorry we had a part in helping him to deceive his grandfather," Danny said. "And I want to ask his forgiveness."

"Big deal!" his cousin snapped. "You know what he's going to think, don't you? He'll wonder how we could be so stupid as to do that!"

"I hope he understands," Danny continued. "I really do. But it doesn't make much difference whether he does or not. The important thing is that I do it and tell him that we won't be coming over to go fishing with him unless we can go to his grandfather's house to pick him up!"

"That's stupid—really stupid! You know that, don't you?"

CHAPTER 10

SOMEBODY'S OUT THERE

Stephen Driscoll helped his grandfather clean the fish and ice them, working hurriedly, but with an outward show of calm and quiet. When they were finished, he got his jacket and started for the canoe.

"Where you goin'?" his grandfather growled.

The boy stopped and turned to face the old man. With difficulty, he kept the anger and resentment from his voice. "Out on the lake—okay?"

"You ain't seein' that Orlis kid again, are you?"

Stephen's temper flared, and for an instant he feared his flaming cheeks would give him away. "No, I ain't seein' Danny Orlis! Does that make you happy?"

Before LeFevre could reply, they were startled by the sound of Peter Starr's jet. It came softly into their hearing at first, drifting in on the back of the gentle breeze. They both looked up as the roar increased. Moments later, the sleek craft appeared around the end of an island, skimming over the water.

"If you've got to know," Stephen bristled, "I was going to see Pete." He waved to the boy in the boat.

The old man nodded and turned away. He didn't like the sight of that boat roaring all over the lake scaring the fish and the birds and anything else that was within a mile of it. But having Stephen with Peter Starr was a sight better than having him with young Orlis. At least the spirits wouldn't be angry because of it.

He made his way down to the icehouse and lowered himself wearily to the bench. With satisfaction, he watched his grandson paddle the canoe away from the dock and start the small motor to head for the jet. By this time, the speedboat was sitting motionless in the water.

Out on the lake, Peter Starr waited until the younger boy reached him. Satisfaction gleamed in his bony features.

"How'd you know I wanted to see you today?"

Stephen shrugged.

"I'm glad you came out. It's about time you and I got together again." He grinned crookedly.

Stephen's cheeks flushed as he looked away quickly.

"Well?" Peter continued. "How about it?"

The younger boy hesitated. He didn't really like being with the owner of the speedboat. Peter was always pushing him to do things he didn't want to do.

"Make up your mind, will you? I haven't got all day."

"Sorry," Stephen said, properly apologetic, "but I've got things I've got to do."

"Like what?"

"Goin' fishing."

"Now don't try to tell me that!" Peter snorted in derision. "The old man's already lifted his nets. I saw you come in an hour or so ago."

"I didn't mean that kind of fishing," Stephen went on. "I meant sport fishing."

"Sounds great to me. Put your canoe over on that island and let's go! We can work out our plans while we're fishing."

Stephen hadn't expected an answer like that. He didn't want to go fishing with Peter. He wanted to be with Danny and Grant, in spite of the trouble he was in with his grandfather because of them. Them and that stupid church, he told himself.

"I–I'd like to go with you," he said, "but I've already promised Danny Orlis I'd go out with him and his cousin. I'm supposed to meet them on the other side of Moose Island." He glanced at his watch. "I'm late now."

Peter's face twisted into a mirthless grin. "What's the deal? Don't that granddad of yours want them around, either?"

The younger boy didn't answer.

"You'd better forget those guys and go with me." He winked broadly. "We've got some talking to do."

"You can go along if you want to," Stephen said quickly.

"With them?" Peter snorted. "No way. I wouldn't be caught dead with that straight arrow! He makes me *sick* just to talk to him!"

Stephen nodded reluctantly. He didn't like to talk about Danny, but Peter was expecting an answer. Almost against his will he found himself parroting his older friend. "Me too. He acts as though he's so much better than anyone else. I get tired of it."

Scorn gleamed in Peter's blue eyes. "Y'know something, Steve?" he went on. "You hang around with that dude and he'll nail you! You'll wind up just like him—scared to do anything that's any fun!"

Stephen swore to show how tough he was. "No way, Man. No way!"

"It's bad! Let me clue you in! I've seen it happen before, lots of times! My own sister used to be a ball! She'd get smashed on booze or spaced out on pot, and she was a riot. Then she went off to college and got into some kind of a religious club or something. You ought to see her now! She's just like Orlis. Won't do anything she used to. Won't even go to parties with her old friends. Says *Jesus* wouldn't want her to." His lips curled contemptuously about the name of Christ.

Stephen noted the time again. "I've got to go," he said. "Orlis promised to give me five bucks if I'd show him a couple of good pike holes, and I can sure use the money."

As he spoke, Stephen realized he had lied again. It seemed as though he was lying all the time now, though he had scarcely noticed it before. What was it the Sunday school teacher had said about that? "God hates a lie."

The words drove deeply within his heart. He had never paid attention to God before. He didn't want to now. But having God hate his lying was something else!

By that time, Peter saw that he was not going to be able to persuade his friend not to go over to see Danny and Grant. "Go ahead," he replied, as though the decision was his to make. "I'll take off and be back in about an hour. That'll give us time to work things out and still let you get home before your granddad gets uptight about your being gone so long."

"I–I'll try to make it," Stephen said in a tone that indicated he really didn't plan to. "But it depends on how long I have to wait on him."

"You'd better be back here," Peter snarled. "I'll be waiting! And I don't like being stood up. Understand?"

Stephen turned and pulled the starter rope. The little three-horse outboard started immediately, whining like so many mosquitoes. He would have put it in gear, but Peter Starr still clutched the canoe, holding it against his side of the speedboat.

"Remember what I said! *One hour?*"

"If I can."

"You'll make it!" Peter added confidently, a hint of warning in his words.

With that, he shoved the canoe away from his own speedy craft, started the jet, and zoomed off, almost swamping the fragile canoe. For a terrifying instant, Stephen was certain he would be swamped. The canoe shipped water dangerously, but with difficulty he managed to remain upright.

Only when the older boy was a speck in the distance did Steve turn and look toward shore. His grandfather wasn't in sight. He hoped that meant the cantankerous old man had gone somewhere so he couldn't see that Peter had sped away alone. If he had, he would wonder why, and there could be trouble. But Stephen couldn't worry about that right then. If the old man asked about it, he would have to think of something fast. He put his motor in gear and headed south across the open water.

It would be just his luck to have had Danny and Grant show up at the island on time and decide that he wouldn't be coming. He didn't want that.

Danny and Grant had appeared at the island rendezvous some time earlier and were disturbed that Stephen hadn't arrived.

"Maybe that granddad of his got his back up and wouldn't let him leave the place this morning," Grant said.

Danny had to agree that was entirely possible, but he didn't think that was the reason for the other boy's absence. "He might have had to wait until he got some work done around the place," he said. "That happens to me all the time."

Grant frowned. "I guess it doesn't make much difference whether he comes or not, if we aren't going fishing with him."

Danny did not reply. He had made up his mind what they had to do. It wasn't going to be easy talking to Stephen. He wouldn't be able to understand why Danny wouldn't meet him at the island anymore, but that didn't matter.

Stephen appeared a few minutes later, apologetic for not being on time.

"That's all right," Danny said. "We just came over to talk to you."

"You mean *you* just came over to talk," Grant blurted. "*I* figured on going fishing!"

"I told you before we left that we were just going to talk to Steve today."

The other boy eyed him suspiciously. "You mean we aren't going fishing?"

"Not today." He cleared his throat. "The fact is, we're not going to be able to go fishing with you anymore unless we can come up to the house to get you."

Stephen's eyes narrowed. "Has that grandfather of mine gotten to you?" he demanded.

"We haven't seen him since we were over to the house the last time," Danny said, "but I've been bothered about the fact that we've been helping you deceive your grandfather when we meet you this way."

"I don't see how you figure that."

"You do it so he won't know you're with us, don't you?"

Stephen paused, staring down at the water. "It's because he's got it in for me! He doesn't want me to do anything that's any fun!"

"When we meet you away from the house, we're helping you lie to him—and we're not doing that anymore."

Stephen could scarcely believe what Danny was saying. "Pete Starr was right!" he stormed. "You think you're so much better than anyone else! Just because you're a *Christian,* you want everybody to believe you're perfect!" He started the motor on his canoe. "I've had it! Don't bother coming around here anymore! I'm sorry I showed you where to catch fish! I'll sure know better the next time!"

When he was gone, Danny glanced at his cousin. "I'm sorry he took it like that. I didn't want to make him mad."

"What did you expect?" Grant exploded. "He thought you were his friend, but he found out you wouldn't even help him stay out of trouble with that bad-tempered old man he has to live with. I don't blame him!"

Stephen was so disturbed that he didn't even wait for Peter Starr to return. He went to the house, pulled the canoe up on shore, and turned it over—aware of the fact that his grandfather was watching from the front door.

"Well, did I get back in time to suit you?" he demanded bitterly.

The old man nodded. "When I saw that Starr kid go off in one direction and you in the other, I figured you were going to meet young Orlis somewhere." He leaned forward slightly, a grin exposing his snaggled teeth. "I was fixing to go out on the lake and have a look, when I seen you come around the island and head for home." His smile broadened. "I'm proud of you, Stephen. I'm right proud of you!"

His grandson cringed inwardly. *What would the old man say if he knew the truth?*

"Everything's going to be fine," the old man said. "Just fine."

Stephen turned from his grandfather and stormed up the hill, his cheeks burning fiercely. That Danny Orlis! he fumed inwardly. He wasn't going to talk the way he had and get away with it! He would get even with him if it was the last thing he did.

He expected Peter Starr to come by again, as he said he would. When they talked briefly earlier in the morning, he indicated he had something important to go over with the young Indian boy. In fact, there was an ominous tone in his voice that made Stephen want to close his ears and slink away. But there had been excitement, too, that quickened his pulse and caused him to look toward the lake from time to time with growing anticipation.

He was somewhat surprised when the afternoon

crept by and there was no sign of Peter. He was still expecting his older friend when his mum called him in for supper. He would not have been surprised had Peter shown up before dark, buzzing by to attract his attention and waiting for him to come out to meet him. But there was no sign of either the jet or its owner.

Stephen went to bed at his usual time, but he was unable to sleep. He was still angry with Danny Orlis. Where did he get the idea he could treat him as though he was the biggest sinner on the Angle? He might not go to church, he told himself, and he didn't do any talking about being a Christian, but he wasn't any worse than most people he knew. And he was a lot better than some. That ought to count for something.

Yet, even as he tried to make himself believe that he was good enough to go to Heaven, he knew that wasn't true. He was a sinner and needed a Savior. He had to confess his sin and put his trust in Jesus if he was to be saved. That's what they said at church that day, and even though he didn't like it, he had to admit he believed them. In his heart he knew he wasn't good enough to be saved. He could never be good enough—no matter how hard he tried.

He was tossing restlessly when he heard the springs in the next bedroom squeak in protest as his grandfather leaped out of bed.

"Stephen!" the old man shouted. "Rachel! Get up quick! Somebody's out there trying to break into our shed!"

CHAPTER 11

ACCUSED

Stephen scrambled out of bed and pulled on his jeans. His hands were trembling, and his heart hammered frantically against his ribs. He had been afraid the thief would hit them since the first time Sherwood came over and told about the robberies.

Anyone who knew his grandfather realized he didn't have much that anyone would want to steal. Most of the furniture in the drafty cabin was handmade or so old and weary it was about to fall apart. They had no electricity, so they had no appliances—not even a television. And the money he got from fishing and trapping scarcely paid for the things he had to buy.

Yet, the items he had that were of value were in demand and easily disposed of. A fifty-horsepower outboard, five dozen traps of various sizes, eight or ten gill nets, a snowmobile, and several drums of gasoline—the sort of things almost anyone who lived in that area could use. The loss of any of them would be disastrous for the elderly Indian.

In the next room, Tom LeFevre had also pulled on his pants and started for the kitchen door. He snatched his rifle from the corner where it stood and dashed out.

"You, out there!" he shouted, though he could see nothing. "Stop right where you are or I'll shoot!"

Rachel and her son crowded up behind the old man, straining to see in the dark of the clouded night.

"Stop or I'll shoot!" LeFevre repeated, his voice quavering.

There was a rustling in the bush, and he fired wildly. The report echoed and reechoed through the breathless hush that had settled over the little clearing with the disappearance of the sun.

"See anything?" he croaked tensely.

"Do you?"

He did not answer directly. "There was somebody out there," he repeated, numb and drained of emotion. "I'd swear it."

"We didn't hear anything, did we, Stephen?" Rachel turned to her son for support. He had been in such a turmoil he hadn't been listening, but he shook his head.

"I didn't hear a thing."

"How could you?" his grandfather blasted. "You were both asleep!"

"How do you know? You didn't see either of us! You don't know nothing about it!"

His mom put a restraining hand on her son's shoulder and shook her head to quiet him. Stephen expected his grandfather to continue the tirade, but he didn't.

"Stephen," he ordered crisply, "get me the flashlight from the kitchen table. I'm goin' out to see if he got anything!"

With LeFevre in the lead—the flashlight in his left hand and the rifle in his right—the trio crept across the grass in the direction of the little shed where the traps and the snowmobile were kept. The yellow beam, fed by a pair of time-weakened batteries, tore a shallow hole in the darkness. It lighted the path they were following and illuminated a narrow patch of grass and weeds on each side.

From time to time, LeFevre raised the shaft of light, but the opaque blackness swallowed it half a dozen steps ahead.

"There's nobody here," Stephen stammered. "We'd just as well go back."

"I tell you I heard *somebody*!" his grandfather roared. "I've lived in these woods all my life. I *know* when I've heard something."

His daughter shivered.

"I–I'm like Stephen," she managed. "There's nothing out here. We'd just as well go back."

"Go ahead if you want to. I'm staying till I find out what it was!"

They had almost reached the shed when Tom LeFevre thrust the flashlight into his grandson's hand.

"Handle this for me. Okay?"

Stephen took the light with trembling fingers and pointed it toward the path ahead.

"Lift it up!" LeFevre ordered. "That thief ain't going to be on the ground in front of us. There. Now to the left. That's better."

All Stephen could see was the corner of the shed, but he did not mention that to his grandfather. If the old man was satisfied with the way he was using the light, that was all that mattered. In a moment, they were close enough to see that the lock on the shed was intact. It still hung, undisturbed, from the hasp.

"What'd we tell you?" Steve exclaimed. "There was nobody out here."

"But I heard him," his grandfather protested. "I hadn't been asleep yet, so I *know* somebody was out here. And it came from this direction."

Stephen swung the light haphazardly about. "It could have been an animal."

"If it was, it was a big one."

The light, in its wandering, rested briefly on a jack pine nearby.

"What's that?" LeFevre asked.

"A tree."

Stephen's grandfather started forward. "Give me that flashlight," he murmured. "I want to have a look."

He took the flashlight and examined a small section of the tree about five feet off the ground.

"Just as I thought," the old man continued. "There *was* somebody out here. He left his calling card."

Stephen and his mom stared at the fresh slashes on the tree, perpendicular to the trunk. They had been made only a short time before. The exposed wood had not had time to darken.

"A bear!" Rachel exclaimed.

Tom LeFevre was visibly relieved. "A bear!" he repeated, chuckling to himself. "I would have sworn I heard a man trying to break into our shed." He paused. "We can go back to the house now. I should have known the loon wouldn't let anybody rob me."

Stephen didn't see how he could give his spirit-helper credit for that, but he didn't say anything. Maybe this would help to get the old man off his back for a while.

They went back to the house and went to bed. The uneasiness that had enveloped Stephen began to ebb. He thought of Danny Orlis and what he had said. He was going to get even with that guy if it was the last thing he did.

* * * *

At the Orlis home later that same evening, Danny awakened suddenly. He lay motionless in bed, listening to the sound of a faint breeze whispering through the branches outside his window. He remained quiet for a time, listening intently. Something had awakened him—a sound that was different from the usual night noises. A flat, jarring sound, like the bumping of heavy metal or wood against wood.

Carefully he raised himself on one elbow and leaned forward in an effort to sort it out and determine its origin. But all was silent once more, save for the light wind, the murmuring of the waves against the shore, and the pleasant croaking of the frogs among the pads along the shore.

Reason told him to go back to sleep, but he couldn't do that—not without checking first. As quietly as possible, he slipped out of bed and dressed. He found the electric lantern he kept on the floor of his closet and tiptoed to the door. As he turned the knob, Grant woke up instantly. He sat upright in bed.

"Where're you going, Danny?" he demanded. "What's up?"

Danny put a warning finger to his lips to keep him from talking too loud. "I thought I heard something outside and was going out to have a look."

"Hang in there a jiff." Grant swung his feet over the side of the bed and got his jeans. "I'll go along."

Together, the two boys stole out of the house as quietly as possible and looked about, swinging the powerful rays of the light from one side to the other, examining the outbuildings carefully.

"Everything *looks* all right," Grant said.

Danny was about to agree when he fixed the harsh beam on the shed where the outboards and snowmobiles were kept. The hasp and the lock were there, but they hung down at a strange angle, and the door was slightly ajar.

He started forward rapidly, his cousin right beside him.

"What're you looking at?" Grant wanted to know.

"Can't you see?" Danny echoed.

By that time, they reached the shed and saw that someone had broken off the lock and had gone inside. As Danny flung the door open, the powerful light chased the darkness from the interior of the small shed. The snowmobiles were there, but their two newest outboards were gone!

"We did have visitors!" Grant exclaimed.

"And they got Dad's two best motors!"

Danny woke his parents, and the four of them checked the shed thoroughly to be sure nothing else was missing. Then they searched the place for clues the thief—or thieves—might have left.

"They came by boat, all right," young Orlis said, pointing to the marks in the mud along the creek bank where a boat had been pulled up.

"But there was only one," Carl Orlis remarked. "At least only one got out of the boat." He pointed to the footprint that revealed that information.

Danny and Grant both stared down at it.

"Did you ever see a footprint like that before?" Danny asked his cousin.

"I'm not sure."

* * * *

Tom LeFevre got up at the usual time, dressed, and made himself a cup of coffee before waking his grandson so they could go out on the lake to lift the nets. The clouds had disappeared, fleeing with the coming of daylight, while the sun was warming the breeze and the rumpled surface of the bay.

"That bear had me fooled last night," he told Stephen. "I was sure we were being robbed."

"Me too."

"But we don't have to worry about that anymore. We've got the loon to take care of us. As long as we–" The words caught in his throat and choked off suddenly. "We–We–"

Stephen's cheeks paled, and his lower jaw sagged. He tried to speak but could not. The padlock and hasp had been pried off and were lying on the ground. The door was ajar.

"There was a thief out here after all!" LeFevre murmured.

"It was all right when we looked last night," Stephen said numbly. "Nobody had disturbed anything."

"He might have been hiding in the bush," the old man continued. He stopped and turned to his grandson. It was as though he was afraid to open the door for fear of what he would find. "Or he may have come back. He might even have returned this morning just before daylight—especially if we scared him off last night."

Stephen pushed the door open and gasped. His grandfather's motor was gone. LeFevre stared at the rack where it should have been.

"The loon was supposed to take care of me and my things," he said helplessly. "I burned tobacco and sweet grass to her and put jewelry and cloth out in the bush as sacrifices, but they didn't do any good. Not a bit of it."

Stephen looked up at the wrinkled face of his grandfather and then away. It wouldn't be long until the old man decided it was *his* fault that his spirit-helper hadn't protected him and his motor. But even that seemed unimportant now. Without the motor, they would have no way of lifting the nets or getting around on the lake, except for the canoe and the three-horse motor. It took forever to go to Danny's. How long would it take to make the long trip to Kenora for supplies? And where would they get the money they needed?

For the first time he began to understand his grandfather's concern.

"What are we going to do now?" he asked.

"Look for clues," LeFevre said, "that would give us a line on who did this to me. Then I'm going to send you over to Customs to have them notify the OPP." Desperation crept into his voice. "We've got to get that motor back. That's all there is to it!"

They went through the shed with care and searched the grounds around it, but found nothing. They were about to give up and get Stephen on his way to Customs when LeFevre cried out triumphantly and bent to pick up a small crowbar about thirty inches long.

"This is what the thief used!" he said, examining it carefully.

"Are you sure?" Stephen asked, his eyes widening.

His grandfather caught the change in his expression. "You ever see this bar before?"

The boy hesitated. He had seen the bar before—he was sure he had. The thought came to him suddenly. This was just what he needed to get back at Danny for treating him like he was such a terrible sinner. This would show him!

The old man grasped Stephen by the arm. "Have you seen it before?"

Stephen nodded, pulling to get away.

"All right! Where?" LeFevre tightened his grasp until his grandson winced. "Where did you see it? Answer me, or I'll break your arm!"

"Danny Orlis had it!" Stephen said.

"Danny Orlis, eh?" the old man exclaimed. "Wait till I get the OPP after him!"

CHAPTER 12

"IT COULDN'T HAVE BEEN DANNY"

Carl Orlis and the boys searched the grounds carefully for some clue that might point to the culprit. The theft had been carried out by one person. That was apparent. They found a number of footprints—both partial and complete. Those leading up to the shed were so faint that they had difficulty making them out. Some of those returning to the boat were the same, but others were sharply indented in the soft ground.

"Whoever made these prints," Carl said firmly, "was carrying something heavy."

"Like an outboard motor?" Danny asked.

"Like an outboard motor. A heavy outboard like our new sixty."

Danny knelt beside one of the footprints, going over it carefully. The mud edges that outlined the tread had been soft when it was first made. Now it was hardening.

"This was made a little while ago," he muttered to himself. "It's already drying out."

Carl Orlis nodded. With that, he pulled himself up and stared out over the placid waters of Pine Creek. The wind was beginning to build, and the surface of the bay was beginning to toss restlessly. In a few minutes, the creek would be affected, and waves would be splashing through the boards on the long dock.

"We've got to get word to the sheriff," he said aloud. "And the wind's coming up. Take the *Scappoose* and go to American Point. They'll radio Roseau for you."

Danny and Grant returned to the shed, got out one of the older motors, and clamped it to the stern of his boat. They filled the tank with mixed gas and pushed away from the dock.

"Think it'll start?" Grant asked doubtfully.

For answer, Danny jerked the starter rope. There was no sound from the aging engine. He squeezed the bulb on the gas hose and tried again. The motor hadn't been used for some time and was difficult to start. He tried a dozen times before it finally caught with a roar that could be heard half a mile away.

"Here we go!" he exclaimed.

"Think it'll get us there?" his cousin wanted to know.

"It always has."

* * * *

Tom LeFevre had sent Stephen to the Customs House two hours earlier. As Danny and Grant were pulling away from the Orlis dock, the OPP were arriving at LeFevre's by helicopter. They came in from Kenora, bucking a stiff wind. The elderly Indian went down to meet them.

"Understand you've had some problems, Mr. LeFevre," the sergeant said.

"Problems?" he echoed. "They stole my best motor. That's what they did! I'll say I've had problems. Plenty of them. But I know who did it!"

The officer acted as though he was about to ask the old man who he suspected but changed his mind. "I'd like to have a look around first," he said. "Then we'll ask some questions."

LeFevre and Stephen went with them to the shed where the break-in occurred. Rachel Driscoll stood in the kitchen doorway, the screen ajar, watching what went on.

"I heard something last night a little while after we went to bed," the old man said as they crossed the lawn. "We got up as quick as we could and went out to have a look. But we couldn't see nothing except the claw marks of a bear on that jack pine. He was a doozy, too. A regular old he-bear!"

The officer examined the shed carefully, noting

the items that had been left and the motor LeFevre said had been stolen.

"You can get it back, can't you?" the fisherman asked plaintively. "I've *got* to have it. Can't get nowheres on the lake if I don't. Besides, you don't have to waste all this time. I already know who did it!"

The policeman did not answer him. Instead he went from the interior of the log building to the door where the padlock had been fastened, examining it carefully.

"Whoever it was pried the hasp off."

"And the bar's right over here," LeFevre said. "Me and my grandson found this crowbar out here early this morning. The thieves dropped it right by the door and forgot to pick it up." He proudly drew himself up. "I found out who it belongs to. My grandson seen it over at the Orlis house the last time he was there. That religious nut's son had it. Find him and you'll find my motor!"

The officer stared at him as though he couldn't believe what he was hearing.

"Surprised you, eh?" LeFevre echoed. "It'll su'prise a lot of people when they find out that the kid of those fanatics who're trying to get everybody saved is a thief!" He chuckled to himself. "Yes, siree, that'll surprise a lot of people."

The officer took out his handkerchief and wrapped it about the bar before picking it up.

"Including me," he said.

"Did you mean what I think you did?"

"I don't know what you thought," the officer replied, picking up the bar and holding it carefully in his hand. "But I'll tell you what I mean. I know Danny Orlis. I've known that kid since he was hanging onto his mum's hand to walk across the floor. I've seen my share of trouble up and down the Angle. In fact, I suppose I've arrested almost every scoundrel in these parts at some time or another. I've never examined any theft where there was one shred of evidence that Danny Orlis was the guilty party. And I've never talked to a victim who even hinted they thought he had stolen anything or done anything wrong.

"I can tell you this much, Mr. LeFevre, Danny's a good boy with a good reputation. I only wish all the kids around here were like him. It'd make my job a lot easier."

Rage twisted the Indian man's features. "You're like all the rest!" he blurted. "You've been taken in by them." LeFevre leaned forward slightly. "Know something? I wouldn't be surprised if that Carl Orlis is in on it, too. The kid could do the stealing, and he could sell it to somebody on the outside—maybe to some of them tourists who are always coming to his place. I'll bet they'd all like to pick up a good outboard motor cheap."

The officer ignored his insistence that Danny Orlis was the thief. "I'll take this bar to Kenora and lift the fingerprints from it," he went on. "That might give me a clue as to who we're looking for."

"Why do you have to do that? I've already told you who the thief is. Go down and arrest him before he sells my motor and gets it down to Minneapolis or someplace like that."

The officer started toward the helicopter with the crowbar in his hand. "I can't do that," he said. "In the first place, the Angle is full of these bars. Every place on the bay has got one or two—maybe more. We would have to have a great deal more evidence than that to arrest someone with a reputation like Danny has. And another thing. They are Americans and are on the other side of the border. I can't go across the line and make an arrest."

"They've got police!" LeFevre fumed. "Get hold of the American authorities, and have them make the arrest."

"It's not as simple as that." He turned back to the distraught commercial fisherman. "Don't get so upset. Your motor was just stolen. Whoever took it hasn't had a chance to get it away from the lake. We've got a very good chance of finding out who stole it and getting it back for you."

The old man shook his head. "You mean you ain't goin' to do nothing?" he demanded. "You ain't even going to *try* to get me my motor? You ain't even goin' to get the Americans to arrest that Orlis kid?"

"Not until somebody shows me some solid evidence that he's the thief." He opened the helicopter door and turned back to the distraught old man.

"You've got things all wrong. I'd trust Danny Orlis with anything I own!"

With that, the pilot motioned LeFevre and Stephen away from the helicopter and started the rotor. It moved slowly at first, gradually picking up speed.

Stephen stood beside his grandfather, disappointment clouding his dark young features. His mind was a jumble of conflicting emotions. He had a certain relief that the police could not go over into Minnesota and arrest the young Christian. But at the same time he was disturbed by their lack of interest in pursuing the matter. He had counted on getting even with Danny for the things he said.

Stephen knew as well as the police officer that Danny wasn't guilty, but that did not make him less determined to get revenge. What Danny said had burned so deeply into the Indian lad's heart that he hadn't been able to sleep. The hurt was so savage that he had to strike out—to make a wild, unreasoning attempt to hurt Danny, to get even.

"We know Danny broke into your shed," he told his grandfather. "Can't the OPP do anything about it? Can't they go over and arrest him?"

"It didn't sound that way," the old man muttered savagely. "But that doesn't mean *we* have to stay away. Get your jacket. We'll borrow Sherwood's boat and motor. He'll be as anxious as we are to have us get over and talk to Carl Orlis." A triumphant smile crinkled his seamed face. "That Orlis is going to find out that he and his kid aren't so much."

Stephen wasn't sure he wanted to go to Angle Inlet with his grandfather. It was one thing to lie about the crowbar. It was quite another to face the one he had lied about—to stand there as he knew he would have to and hear his grandfather repeat the lie. But he had to go along. There was no way of getting out of it.

They hurried through the woods to Ivar Sherwood's and borrowed his boat.

"You sure about young Orlis?" the neighbor asked when LeFevre told him about the theft and explained the reason for needing the boat. "You know, he's never been in any trouble."

"If I wasn't sure, we wouldn't be going over there," the old man retorted. "Stephen, here, seen that very same crowbar over at the Orlis place. The same bar as we found outside my shed this morning."

Ivar went down to the lakeshore and helped them launch his boat and get the engine started. LeFevre noted that the gas tank was full but said nothing about it. If he caught the thief, he figured Sherwood ought to be grateful enough to put out a little gas. He wouldn't have to worry about losing any of his stuff.

"What're we going to do when we get there?" Stephen asked.

His grandfather acted as though he hadn't heard. His sunken, watery eyes were fixed on the passageway that led between two islands and the open bay beyond. He hadn't answered the boy because he didn't know what he could do. The robbery had taken place on the Canadian side of the border. If the police couldn't go into the States to make an arrest, the Minnesota police would not be able to arrest an American for a crime that happened in Canada. At least not without the right papers—and it would probably take months to get them. It was stupid how the laws protected the thief. It made him wish he could take the matter into his own hands. He'd solve it quickly enough.

They were leaving the islands behind them when he saw a loon winging slowly over the water ahead. Everything was going to work out all right, he told himself with a smile. His spirit-helper was going to see to it.

As Stephen and his grandfather approached Pine Creek and the Orlis place, the sheriff was just finishing work on plaster casts of the two best footprints. The plaster of paris had dried, and he had lifted the casts from their resting places.

"They're perfect," he said with satisfaction. "Perfect. Clues like these can be invaluable."

Danny and Grant watched as he wrapped them in tissue paper and put them in a box.

"Danny," the sheriff said, straightening, "would you mind running to the house and telling Joe I'm ready to go back?"

Danny scampered off. When he was gone, the officer turned to Mr. Orlis.

"I don't know what to make of this, Carl. I'll be sending a man in to do some checking. And I'll get in touch with the Canadians, just in case the thief came from there."

"Good enough."

They were all at the dock where the float plane was tethered when Tom LeFevre and his grandson came up.

"You the police?" the old man demanded, noting the sheriff's uniform.

"That's right."

"Then you've already got him!" He grinned broadly. "When I saw the loon this morning I knew everything was going to work out."

By this time everyone was eyeing him curiously.

"Did you find out what he did with my motor?"

Sheriff Reddington frowned. "I don't believe I know what you're talking about."

"Sure you do. You're here to arrest that Orlis kid, ain't you?"

"Why would I do that?"

"Because he was over to my place last night and stole my outboard. That's why!"

Danny's cheeks paled, and his breath came in quick, shallow gasps. He stared at his dad and Sheriff Reddington—then at the elderly Indian man. It was the first time anybody had ever accused him of stealing. He knew he wasn't guilty, but how could he prove it? What could he say?

"I–I didn't steal anything!" he protested lamely. "I didn't even leave the house last night."

"That's right," his dad said. His mom and cousin nodded their agreement.

"Here are three witnesses who say he didn't go anywhere last night," Sheriff Reddington told LeFevre.

"What could you expect from *them?*"

"Oh, that isn't all. Carl Orlis was also robbed—probably by the same thieves. Danny couldn't have done it because their motors were also stolen. He wouldn't have had a good fast way to get over to your place and back. Besides, he wouldn't have robbed his own dad."

"You say that because they're so religious!"

"I say that because it's true." The sheriff turned deliberately away from the old man to speak to Danny. "Don't worry about this. I *know* it isn't true, and so will anyone else who knows you."

"Is that all you're going to do?" LeFevre shouted.

"For now. I've known this boy a long time. He's not involved in whatever's going on around these parts. I don't want to hear any more about it. Understand?"

The old Indian glared at the officer. "You're as bad as the OPP. They wouldn't believe me either! But I'll prove you're wrong." He turned away abruptly and put a hand on his grandson's shoulder. "There's no use telling them about Danny's crowbar you found over at our shed. They ain't going to believe anything we tell 'em. But I ain't done yet. I'm going home and summon the loon to help me prove Danny's guilty. Then they'll find out the truth!"

"What was that about a crowbar?" Carl Orlis asked.

"Don't give it another thought," the sheriff said. "You know yourself that everybody's got those crowbars. I must have three or four myself, and they all look alike."

Before the sheriff left, Danny approached him and asked if he could buy some of the plaster of paris he had left.

"What would you be doing with it?"

"I'd like to see if I can make some of those casts."

"Sure thing. Take what's left." He thrust the bag into the boy's hands.

CHAPTER 13

EXPOSED

Danny and his cousin watched the sleek Cessna taxi toward the bay and take off.

"That was scary!" Grant exclaimed. "It was lucky for you that the sheriff's a good friend of your dad's."

"How come?"

"He'd have arrested you for stealing old LeFevre's motor."

"That wouldn't have stopped Mr. Reddington if he had believed I was guilty," Danny claimed. "He does his job without thinking about whether or not he's dealing with friends."

"Then it's a good thing you've got a good reputation," Grant said. "I guess it pays for a guy to behave himself."

"It does, for a fact."

"I know this much. From here on out I'm going to work at it. That was neat the way he wouldn't even listen to LeFevre when the old man started accusing you of stealing from him. I'd like to have a reputation like that."

"There's one good way to get all the help you need to live a clean life," Danny said. "If you confess your sin and put your trust in Christ, He will help you to live the way you should."

Grant hesitated. The muscles about his mouth tightened, and for a moment he did not speak. "I'd have to think on that," he said quietly. "I don't know if I'm quite ready."

"Don't wait too long," Danny told him.

When the plane taking the sheriff back to Roseau was out of sight, the boys set to work. They got a large coffee can from the trash, mixed about half the plaster of paris with clean water, and poured the thin paste into the footprints of the thief.

"Now," Danny said, "we'll have to wait until they dry before we try to take them out."

Mrs. Orlis called them to dinner. By the time they were able to check the casts, they were ready to be removed. Danny cut the mud away from one side with his knife and got the blade under the layer of plaster of paris. He broke the first cast but managed to get the second out in one piece.

"That's almost as good a job as Sheriff Reddington did," Grant said.

"A couple of corners didn't get filled, but you can sure see what kind of tennis shoe made that print."

"Nikes?"

Danny nodded. "Any idea of anyone we know who wears Nikes?"

"There's only one guy I've met since I've been here who can afford them."

"That's exactly what I was thinking." Danny got to his feet, holding the cast carefully in his right hand. "We'd better go over and pay him a visit."

Grant's cheeks paled and concern leaped to his eyes. "Hey, Man! He's a lot bigger than we are. What if he doesn't *like* our nosing around?"

"There're two of us," young Orlis said. "That ought to count for something. Besides, I don't plan on telling him why we're there. I just want to get a look at those shoes of his."

"You make it sound so easy," Grant put in, doubt creeping into his voice. "Pete's sharp. And if he's in this mess the way we think he is, he's going to be suspicious. What if he figures it out?"

Danny grinned. "Then we'll think of something else."

They asked permission from Mrs. Orlis to go out on the lake, gassed up the *Scappoose*, and pulled away from the dock.

"What're we going to do if we find out he is our man?"

Danny was silent for a moment. "I've been wondering about that myself. We could go to the OPP with this cast and see if they would follow up on it. If they won't, I don't know what we'll do."

"I can think of something right now," Grant muttered. "We can stay home."

"And let him get away with it?" Danny echoed. "No way."

* * * *

Across the bay on the Canadian side, LeFevre and Steve were at the house after returning Sherwood's boat.

"I'm going to catch a ride up to Kenora," the old man stormed. "I ain't lettin' Orlis and that kid get away with this. I'm goin' to talk to somebody and get action—even if I have to go all the way to Winnipeg."

"Think it'll do any good?" Stephen asked.

"You *bet* it will! I'll raise enough stink to get *some* kind of action." He started toward the house but turned back to his grandson. "Get the canoe gassed up while your mum fixes us a few sandwiches to take along."

"Where are we going?" Stephen asked uneasily. He was always wary when that tone crept into his grandfather's voice.

"Over to Customs, of course. Those officers hang out there every time they come in. I'll catch me a ride with them." He chuckled at his own cleverness.

They left the dock in a few minutes and made their way to the Customs House several miles to the east. It was not long after noon, and the OPP helicopter was still in the yard. The officers were sitting at the kitchen table with the Customs officer and his wife. They were irritated by LeFevre's appearance but agreed to take him to Kenora when they went. Ordinarily, they would not have provided him transportation, but this time he had legitimate business with the department.

"You'll have to wait until we're ready to leave," the sergeant said. "We've got some business to attend to."

LeFevre snorted in derision. "It looks like it," he retorted.

Anger flecked the officer's eyes, but his voice was even and calm. "We have some government business to discuss," he went on. "You can wait for us outside."

Stephen left his grandfather on the small island near the helicopter and made his way toward home. He didn't know why he detoured to Peter Starr's. His grandfather had ordered him to go straight home and reminded him again as he got into the canoe and shoved off. Yet, when he reached the place where he would have passed the Starrs' big summer home, he impulsively turned in.

He was going to tell Peter about finding the crowbar and how he had told everyone it belonged to Danny Orlis. His older friend would think that was a blast. He wouldn't have to say that nobody believed it except his grandfather. He was grinning to himself as he headed the canoe toward the Starr acreage on the mainland.

The jet boat was tied to one side of the long dock. A strangely familiar craft was pulling in to tie up on the windward side. He saw that there were two guys in the other boat. As he drew closer, he realized who it was.

Danny and Grant! What were they doing here?

Peter Starr must have seen the *Scappoose* from some distance away. He had come out of the house and covered half the distance to the dock by the time they were tied up.

Stephen was also watching them with growing uneasiness. For a minute, he thought of veering off and continuing toward home, but Peter recognized him and motioned him ashore. Almost against his will, he continued toward them. They were still in the boat, as though undecided as to whether they should leave or stay. He hoped they would shove away from the dock and go before Peter got down to them.

He was not alone in that. Grant agreed with him.

"Think we ought to go through with this?" he murmured under his breath.

Danny grinned at him and winked.

"It's not funny," his cousin exploded.

"What's not funny?" a voice demanded from the dock.

The boys looked up to see Peter Starr peering down at them. Grant's cheeks flushed, and it was all he could do to keep from looking away quickly.

"What isn't funny?" Peter repeated.

"It's a private joke," Danny said.

By that time, Stephen had joined them.

"What happened?" Peter asked, turning his attention to the newcomer. "Is the old man away or sick in bed?"

"As a matter of fact, he's on his way to Kenora. We got ripped off last night. Somebody stole our best outboard."

"They hit you, too, didn't they, Danny?" the older boy asked.

"How did you know that?" Danny asked quickly. "The sheriff just left after flying up to investigate. Nobody around here has had time to know about it."

Peter's cheeks darkened, and he was obviously flustered. "I–I heard it on the radio," he said lamely.

"That couldn't be," Danny persisted. "Sheriff Reddington didn't give out any information before he came up here, and he hasn't had time to get home and talk to any reporters."

"He must have," Peter blustered. "I just heard about it on the news. If you don't believe it, come in and ask my old man! He'll tell you."

Danny didn't believe him, but he didn't press the matter. He changed the subject abruptly.

"Nice tennis shoes you've got there, Pete."

"Tennis shoes?" His features wrinkled curiously. "Oh, you mean *runners*. Yeah, they're Nikes. Only kind I ever wear. The old man brought me three new pairs a couple of weeks ago." He extended his foot and turned it proudly. "Nice, eh?"

"That's a funny tread it's got," Danny put in, grasping Peter's foot and turning it so both he and Grant could get a good look at the pattern carved in the rubber sole.

Peter jerked away. "There's nothing funny about them," he muttered. "They're just the regular Nike markings. Not every guy's got shoes like this. They cost a lot of money."

Danny only had time to catch a quick glimpse of the pattern on the expensive tennis shoes, but it was enough. The markings in the plaster cast were exactly the same. He didn't have to put them together to know that.

"This is really interesting, Pete," he said, unwrapping one of the plaster casts and showing it to him. "The tread of your Nikes and this cast are exactly alike."

Grant sucked in his breath sharply as fright leaped to Peter's narrowing eyes. " Where'd you get that?" he demanded.

"That's another funny thing. We found this footprint at our place this morning after we were robbed."

Stephen Driscoll, who had gotten out of his canoe and was standing nearby, looked quickly at Peter.

"What's that supposed to mean?" the older boy blustered.

Before Danny could answer, the air was filled with noise as the OPP helicopter zoomed over the trees and settled on the lawn. The boys stared in bewilderment as the rotor shut off and the passenger's door opened. The sergeant climbed out, followed by Tom LeFevre.

"There he is!" the elderly Indian shouted, pointing at Danny. "He's in Canada! You can arrest him now!"

"I don't have a warrant."

"That don't make no difference! I'll sign the papers. I'll sign anything you want me to, only don't let him get away!" He turned to his grandson. "We were on our way to Kenora when I spotted that Orlis boat at the dock and made 'em stop. Now we'll show that Carl Orlis what his kid is like!"

"I've got something to show you, Officer," Danny said calmly. He went over and handed him the plaster cast of the footprint they had found in the mud on the shore of Pine Creek. "Sheriff Reddington gave me the plaster of paris to make this cast after he made one just like it for himself."

"Tell me about it."

"Don't pay any attention to him," Peter broke in, sweat pearling his forehead. "He's got it in for me and is trying to get even, that's all." As he spoke, he deliberately shuffled forward to hide his Nike shoes from view.

The officer moved the fish box so he could see the kind of shoes the older boy was wearing. He made him hold one up so he could compare the imprint of the sole. He nodded.

"Very interesting. And you say that your place was robbed last night. Right?"

Danny nodded. "Dad's best motor was taken."

"Take off your left shoe," the officer ordered.

Twin spots of color leaped to Peter's cheeks. "I don't have to," he blustered. "You're not going to pin anything on me!"

The officer read him his rights, and he realized that he would have to do as he was told. Carefully the officer placed the shoe in the cast.

"It's the right tread design and the right size," he said. "The footprint was made by this shoe. I'd stake my life on it."

Tom LeFevre glared at Peter Starr. "I just remembered something, Officer," he said, his tone changing. "I seen footprints like that around my place, too."

"You're lying, Old Man!"

"We can go over and take a look," Stephen's grandfather said firmly. "I know right where they are! In that soft mud and grass west of my dock!"

"I think this is all the evidence we'll need. Come on, Starr. You're under arrest."

"You'll get my motor back for me?" the old Indian asked.

"We'll get your motor and the one Carl Orlis lost. I'm sure Peter is going to be happy to tell us where they are when we get to Kenora!"

"My dad won't let you take me to jail," the boy protested.

"We'll see about that."

Tom LeFevre did not apologize to Danny. That was not his way. He started for the canoe. "Comin', Stephen?"

"I–I think I'll come with Danny and Grant later."

The old man nodded and pushed the canoe into the water. When he was gone, his grandson turned to Danny. "I did something terrible," he said. "I lied about that crowbar. I told my grandfather it was yours when I–I knew it wasn't."

"Why did you do that?" Danny asked curiously.

"I wanted to get back at you for telling me that I'm a sinner and need a Savior."

"We all do. You, me, Grant—everybody."

"But not like me. Know something?" he asked, holding up a thumb and forefinger a quarter of an inch apart. "I came that close to being with Peter last night when he stole those motors. He's been after me to go with him. Said he needed a guy to stand watch and whistle if someone was coming. I didn't want to, but I was afraid he'd think I was chicken if I didn't. If he'd come back, I'd have gone with him. I know it now. And I'd be on my way to Kenora too."

"We can thank God for that," Danny said. "He must have wanted to give you one more chance to confess your sin and accept Christ as Savior."

There was a brief silence.

"Do–do you suppose I could *ever* have people think of me the way they do you? They just *know* you're not going to get into trouble with the police."

"I can't take credit for that," Danny answered. "It's because I've turned my life over to Christ."

Still Stephen hesitated. "I could never live the way you do. I couldn't be that good."

"I can't either," Danny assured him. "Without God's help, I'd be in all sorts of trouble. But He not only will save you, He'll help you to live the way you should."

The Indian boy understood at last. "What do I do?" he asked.

"If you really mean business with God, we'll pray, asking Him to forgive you and save you from sin."

"Sounds good," Stephen replied.

"Pray for me, too," Grant broke in.

Rejoicing, Danny bowed his head with them both. It was wonderful to have his cousin and their friend trust Christ as Savior.

THE DANNY ORLIS SERIES

The Danny Orlis series, by Bernard Palmer, delivers a blend of adventure, mystery, and suspense through various settings—from the Canadian wilderness to Guatemalan jungles. Danny Orlis, an adept outdoorsman, skilled athlete, and committed Christian, employs his quick thinking, calm bravery, and biblical solutions to confront everyday problems and hair-raising dangers. Early stories focus on Danny navigating school life, sports, and outdoor challenges, while in later books, Danny and his wife Kay provide wisdom and guidance to youngsters facing lifelike situations and challenges. Having sold over two million copies, this series has made Palmer a renowned author in Christian youth literature. Palmer is also the author of the Felicia Cartright series and various other series for Christian youth.

AVAILABLE FROM WWW.ANEKOPRESS.COM